AIRBORNE

The Triumph and Struggle of
MICHAEL JORDAN

by Jesse Kornbluth

MACMILLAN BOOKS FOR YOUNG READERS · NEW YORK

Copyright © 1995 by Jesse Kornbluth

Macmillan Books for Young Readers
An imprint of Simon & Schuster Children's Publishing Division
Simon & Schuster Macmillan
1230 Avenue of the Americas
New York, New York 10020

Designed by Joseph Rutt

The text of this book is set in Palatino.

Printed and bound in the U.S.A.

First edition

10 9 8 7 6 5 4 3 2 1

Library of Congress Cataloging-in-Publication Data

Kornbluth, Jesse.
    Airborne : the triumph and struggle of Michael Jordan / by Jesse
Kornbluth. — 1st ed.
        p. cm.
    Includes bibliographical references.
    ISBN 0-02-750922-2
    1. Jordan, Michael, 1963 – .   2. Basketball players — United
States — Biography.   I. Title.
    GV884.J67K64   1995   796.323'092–dc20   [B]   94-12553
Summary: A biography of Michael Jordan, one of the world's finest and
most popular athletes.

For Georgia and Nicholas Tapert,
two high scorers

ACKNOWLEDGMENTS

This book began as a long profile for *Vanity Fair*. While that piece wasn't published, I am grateful for the magazine's support during those intense months of research.

Michael's team of representatives and schedulers at FAME in Washington, D.C.—David Falk, Curtis Polk, and the inimitable Barbara Allen—couldn't have been more generous with their time and insight. At Nike, I spoke extensively with Phil Knight, Howard White, and Dusty Kidd; I'm particularly grateful to Tinker Hatfield for allowing me to sit in on a design meeting. Outside Nike, I was instructed by Sonny Vaccaro, Rob Strasser, Peter Moore, and Julie Strasser. Jerry Reinsdorf, owner of the Bulls, and Steve Schanwald, his key marketing executive, were gracious and candid. Sal Scamardo of CBS/Fox stocked my shelves with Michael's videos. On the media side, David Breskin and John Horan were especially helpful; Jim Riswold illuminated Nike advertising for me. Anne Armstrong of the Michael Jordan Foundation arranged for me to meet some Chicagoans who benefit from Michael's fund-raising efforts; I was humbled by Betty Greer, principal of the Edward Hartigan School, and by her student Jermone Hale. And I was privileged to meet Deloris and James Jordan; their candor and humor helped me to understand their son better.

As ever, I am indebted to my literary agents, Kathy Robbins and Elizabeth Mackey; writers who haven't been encouraged and prodded by Elizabeth can't know what those words really mean.

At Macmillan, "thanks" doesn't begin to suggest my gratitude to Judith Whipple and Leslie Ward. Their understanding that Michael was, in his way, a significant American artist made this book possible; their care throughout made this book more worthy of its subject. Soyung Pak took on the editing chores midway through the project, and brought it home so deftly it sometimes seemed that she had invented it.

The home team usually wonders how I choose my subjects. Not this time. Annette Tapert and her children, Georgia and Nicholas, were fans from beginning to end, offering many editorial suggestions and constantly proposing field trips to basketball games.

My biggest thanks, of course, are reserved for Michael Jordan. In a busy season when he said no to almost everyone with a tape recorder, he said yes to me. His patience was matched by his directness—and his cooperation made everyone else more cooperative. I can easily see why, when the game was on the line, he was the man everyone looked to.

INTRODUCTION

THE FIRST TIME I saw Michael Jordan, he was playing golf in Dallas, Texas. It was a gray winter's day. He was alone. But he looked completely at peace with himself.

"How many holes?" I asked him, when we sat down at breakfast the next morning.

"Thirty," Michael said, with a big smile. "A good day."

The last time I saw Michael Jordan, he was in Portland, Oregon. A few weeks had passed. Once again, he was alone. But this time he was miserable.

"I was ready to go home five days ago," he said. "This is unbelievable: sixteen days on the road. My wife even left. She was going to stay and keep me company, but she couldn't take it. She hopped on a midnight plane. I was envious."

I thought Michael was unhappy mostly because his

team still had another hard week to go on their longest road trip of the year. But as I looked back at my transcript of that interview, I realized he was equally distressed about situations that weren't going to change when he returned to his own bed in Chicago. He was weary of the spotlight. He was angry with reporters who seemed to care more about his private life than his prowess with a basketball. He was tired of being blamed for everything from kids killing one another over sneakers to inner-city children eating at the fast-food restaurant chain he endorses. Most of all, he was running out of challenges.

"I'm at the stage of my career when it's tough to move up—I can only maintain and be consistent," he told me. "I've set such high standards for myself that I lose a little bit of the joy as I move on. And I miss my family a lot. That's why, when it's time to walk away from the game, I know I can do it. I want to watch my children grow. When they start school and their most productive years come, I want to be there for them. I won't have any regrets. When I walk away, I want—if I can—to have a low-key lifestyle."

Michael Jordan said that in early February of 1993. His plan, he told me, was to leave professional sports in 1996. But his motivation didn't last that long. A few months later, during the play-off series against New York, Michael was criticized for driving to Atlantic City on the night before a game to gamble. Then a former golf partner published a book claiming that he and Michael had bet on their games—and that Michael had, in a matter of days, lost $1.3 million.

Despite all the controversy, Michael led the Chicago Bulls to yet another championship. But he found little joy in that. "Winning a third straight championship," he said, "was the hardest thing I've ever done on the basketball court." And then, in midsummer, his father was shot to death at a rest stop on a North Carolina highway.

After that blow, it didn't matter to Michael that he was the only man ever to be voted the Most Valuable Player in a championship series three times in a row. He didn't care that he had averaged forty-one points—another record— in the process. It meant almost nothing that, because of him, this championship series had the highest television ratings in history. In the weeks after his father's funeral, it became clear to him that he just didn't care as much as he used to. And so, although he was only thirty years old, he concluded that it was time to retire.

"I have nothing more to prove in basketball," he announced to two hundred reporters and a dozen television crews at a press conference on October 6, 1993. While he insisted that his decision had nothing to do with his father's death or the pressure he felt from the media, he did say the murder made him realize how short life is and how quickly it can end.

Everybody from President Clinton to Magic Johnson

had an opinion about Michael's unexpected retirement. What was most astounding, of course, was the simple fact that the greatest of all basketball players had quit long before his skills showed the slightest sign of fading. "Nobody has ever left that way," Mike Lupica noted in the *New York Daily News*. "Nothing like this has ever happened in sports."

But then, there had never been a career like Michael Jordan's.

A few years ago, when Chinese high school students were asked to name the people they most admired, two names topped the list. One was inevitable: Chou En-lai, the former chairman of the Communist Party in China. The other was Michael Jordan, identified by many students as a star athlete for an American sports team called the Chicago Red Oxen.

More recently, high school students in Australia were asked to name their favorite athlete. In a country devoted to English games, the winner was not a rugby or soccer player. It was Michael Jordan.

Michael has never been to China or Australia. But his appeal is global—like the soccer star Pele or the boxer Muhammad Ali, his name stands alone as the ultimate champion in his sport. Veteran basketball fans loved to watch him because he was the most complete player the game has ever seen, as brilliant on defense as he was when he brought the ball to the net and scored. Those who didn't care much for basketball but who were mesmerized by him mostly raved about his shooting.

For Michael seemed to do something that eluded all other players—fly. Driving to the foul line, he could launch himself and glide a dozen feet before slamming the ball home. Surrounded by opponents, he could propel himself heavenward until the defenders fell away and, alone, he floated above the rim. Best of all, when one of the giants of the game would rise to meet him, he could shift the ball from hand to hand, change course in mid-flight, and still score.

It wasn't only the fans who thought that Michael's career was one long highlight film. Players and coaches were just as enthusiastic. "Everyone talks about me and Larry Bird," Magic Johnson said. "Really, there's Michael, and then there's everyone else." Larry Bird, awed by Jordan's sixty-three-point performance in a play-off game, told reporters that "He's God, disguised as Michael Jordan." Chuck Daly, who coached the American "Dream Team" in the 1992 Olympics, said, "I had twelve great players on that team, but there was one who was able to raise it to another level." Even Pat Riley, the peerless coach who led the Los Angeles Lakers to more championships than any team in the 1980s, bluntly calls Michael "the greatest player on the planet."

*   *   *

Michael's genius as an athlete is only a small part of his enormous appeal. For in the process of becoming a sports legend, he became bigger than basketball. He did not plan this—he just came along at the right time, with the right kind of personality.

And so Michael Jordan, basketball star, became Michael Jordan, marketing phenomenon. "His line of products sells in excess of $200 million a year—he's 5 percent of our earnings," reports Phil Knight, chairman of Nike. One out of every six basketballs sold in America is a Wilson that bears his signature. Gatorade pays him $18 million over ten years to be its spokesperson—about what it pays the National Football League to be its official drink. Because of him, about 40 percent of all the NBA merchandise sold each year bears the logo of the Chicago Bulls. His first video, released in 1989, is the most successful tape in the history of sports. He is the only athlete ever to be featured on boxes of Wheaties cereal a dozen times.

When you add them all up, Michael is unquestionably the endorsement king of all time, earning about $35 million a year from American companies—seven times more per year than he earned playing for the Chicago Bulls. Thanks to that advertising and the increasingly widespread broadcasting of basketball, he has become better known than Pele or Ali ever had a chance to be: According to the *World Almanac*, Michael was, for the last six years of his career, the most popular human alive.

In one of the many commercials featuring Michael's radiant smile and breathtaking shot making, art imitates life when a child sings he wants to "be like Mike."

But which Michael Jordan?

Is it the athlete who played just as hard in practice as he did in games because he could never forget that as a fifteen-year-old, he was cut from his high school basketball team? Is it the superstar who is so famous that when his team traveled to other cities, he couldn't safely leave his hotel room? Is it the businessman who had to learn about business one deal at a time?

Is it the competitor who loves challenges so much that he would, a friend says, bet on raindrops rolling down a window? Is it the husband and father whose career takes him away from his family? Or is it the celebrity who discovered that more and more reporters see nothing wrong in investigating the most private regions of a star's life?

All of those people exist inside Michael Jordan, but you don't usually meet them in the books and articles that are written about him. Early in 1993, I decided I wanted to look at this complex man in a way that embraced all those facets of his character. And so I arranged to interview Michael, his family, his friends, and his business associates.

The Michael Jordan I found is someone I've never met in the articles and books I had read—a proud African-American who's eager to work hard for the good things that white America has to offer but doesn't want to sacrifice his dignity in order to get them. Such a man has no role models; he must make his way by himself. Michael feels that isolation intensely: "My life has been an education. You can't teach what I'm learning. There are no classes to prepare you, no books to read or lessons to study."

But in making his way, Michael relied on elements that are common to most success stories: working hard, mastering fundamentals, building self-confidence, staying in school, honoring parents, living cleanly, and maintaining humility. Those elements suggest it's his fans, not the superstar, who most enjoy the flash and the glory—for Michael, life seems long on struggle, short on glamour. " 'Be like Mike?' " he asks, with a gleam in his eye. "For a few days, maybe you'd like that. But live it every day . . ."

This book explores how it has felt to be Michael Jordan for thirty-two years. It offers no neat conclusion. Michael is too young; his future is too uncertain. It is entirely possible—despite the indelible stamp he has already left on sports—that his greatest challenges are still ahead of him.

CHAPTER ONE

Michael Jordan always wore his blue University of North Carolina shorts under his Chicago uniform, so most people believe he was born in North Carolina. In fact, he was born in Brooklyn, New York, on February 17, 1963. Although he did more than any other recent player to bring the flashy New York school-yard style of basketball into the professional game, he didn't learn that in Brooklyn—his family moved to North Carolina soon after he was born.

When Michael was a child, it was far from obvious that he would become great at anything. The second youngest of Deloris and James Jordan's five children, Michael didn't grow up with many material advantages. His father was the son of a sharecropper, who started out operating a forklift for General Electric and progressed to become a supervisor. His mother raised the children, and then, when they were all in school, started working at a bank, where she moved up from a teller's window to become head of customer service. The Jordans worked hard and long, but with all those children, they were more concerned with survival than with prosperity: It wasn't until Michael was sixteen years old that he got his first bicycle.

Fortunately for Michael, Deloris and James were loving parents who wanted only the best for their children. "Our kids were our life," Deloris Jordan explains. "PTA, the band, the Boy Scouts—this was how we spent our free time as a family. Every teacher they had knew us. When I went for my job interview at the bank, I told them, 'My kids come first.' So on afternoons of games or activities, I'd work during my lunch hour and leave early."

James Jordan was just as involved with his family. When Michael was seven, James bought a large lot in Wilmington, a coastal city of forty-eight thousand people, and built a split-level brick house on it. Then, because all his children liked sports, he cleared the backyard and created a basketball court—a real thrill for young Michael, who had been shooting junior-sized balls into a trash can.

The Jordan home was fun-loving, but it was also very disciplined. "I saw my mother and father accept the challenge of raising five kids," Michael says. "They both worked two and three jobs. My father never sent a car to a mechanic. If he needed a repair, he'd do it himself. He might screw it up, the engine might drop out, but he'd try. And my mother, she managed the budget for the house and stretched a dollar as far as it could be stretched."

James Jordan expected his sons to help him when he worked on the family car or fixed a toaster. They could always tell when their father was deeply involved in one of these projects—he would open his mouth and let his tongue hang out. When Michael started playing basketball in earnest, he would imitate his father and let his tongue flop out as he jumped to take a shot.

That dangling tongue was about the only way young Michael took after his father. With his head under the hood of his car, for example, James Jordan would ask Michael to hand him a wrench. Michael would seem not to know what he was talking about. "Go in with the women," his father would say. "Learn how to do the dishes." And Michael would shrug and go inside.

"I was lazy as a kid," Michael confesses. "I sometimes got in trouble because I didn't look for summer jobs. I didn't obey my parents and didn't do my schoolwork. I clowned around a lot, picking on people and cutting classes. I just wanted to play ball. And since I didn't work, I didn't have any spending money. But that was all right. All I ever needed was sneakers."

From the beginning, his mother knew why Michael avoided all labor: "If you gave Michael half a dollar to mow the yard, he'd give it to someone else to do the work so he could play sports." But his parents came to understand that Michael's love of athletics wasn't the whole story—this child also enjoyed testing their limits. "If we told him the stove was hot, he'd touch it," James Jordan recalled. "If there was a wet-paint sign, he'd have to make sure it really was wet."

When Michael was eight, serious trouble came to his city. Late in 1971, African-American students and community leaders decided that the white-dominated government of Wilmington had arranged school desegregation in a way that guaranteed black children a second-class education. So they boycotted the public schools and demonstrated at City Hall.

Soon there was violence between blacks and whites. On February 2, 1972, someone fired shots into the church that the protesters were using as their headquarters. That week, a police officer shot and killed a black teenager who was reportedly carrying a shotgun. Finally, as a white-owned grocery burned, police claimed that protesters inside the church fired on them.

With the help of witnesses who were later proved to be unreliable or untruthful, the district attorney convinced a jury of ten white people and two African-Americans to convict ten blacks—eight of them teenagers—for arson and attempted murder. When they were sentenced to terms of twenty-four years, the world was shocked. The convicted protesters became known as "the Wilmington Ten," and civil rights organizations around the world condemned the city for its harsh treatment of its African-American citizens.

Five years later, the Wilmington Ten were freed and the case was thrown out. But in 1972, the violence and injustice made a vivid impression on young African-Americans like Michael Jordan. "Sure, I felt the impact," Michael says. "There was a lot of racism in that town. There's still a lot. My parents lived through it all. They maintained their belief in equality for all races, but they also retained their memories of that problem—and they instilled that in me and in my brothers and sisters. Their message was, 'Yeah, there's a lot of racism, and you should always keep it in the back of your head, but try to be as level as possible and try not to see one race one way or the other.' "

That was a tough assignment for a boy who was sensitive to even little insults—like the taunts that other students sometimes hurled at him because his ears stuck out. "One day, when Michael got on the school bus and took a seat up front, a white girl who considered that seat her own told him to get up," Deloris Jordan recalls. "When he didn't, she spit on him and called him 'nigger.' So he hit her."

Michael was suspended from school for that. His parents didn't blame him, but Deloris repeated what she often said: "Outside this door, all sorts of things will happen. Don't let it affect you. If people call you nigger, that's their ignorance."

Although he was bright and sharp tongued, Michael wasn't a good student in those years. He was too busy playing sports. And for him, that mostly meant baseball.

In those days, there was an unwritten law in Wilmington that said white kids played baseball and black kids played basketball, but Michael loved baseball too much to pay attention to that. He and his best friend, a white boy named David Bridgers, played on a Little League team that almost made it to the Little League World Series. In the key play-off game, Jordan pitched a two-hitter—but his team lost, 1-0. A year later, he was one of only three blacks on a team in the Babe Ruth League that played on a field located in an all-white neighborhood. "He wasn't afraid to stand up for himself," his coach says. "He didn't take anything from them."

In any athletic contest, Michael didn't have to put up with many insults—he was too good for that. "My favorite childhood memory, my greatest accomplishment was when my team won the state championship and I got the Most Valuable Player award," he has said. "I batted over .500, hit five home runs in seven games, and pitched a one-hitter to get us into the championship game. That was the first big thing I accomplished in my life, and you always remember the first."

Baseball was his first love because he was short. Basketball was a sport he played mostly on his backyard court. James Jordan had put a net at each end of the yard, and, after school, his sons played there against neighborhood kids. On Saturdays, they sometimes played all day. Even the rain didn't stop them.

Michael's favorite kind of basketball was one-on-one, with his brother Larry as his opponent. Larry was just a year older, but he was taller, more talented, and fiercely competitive. "Larry used to beat me all the time," Michael says. "I'd get mad, and we'd fight. He created determination in me."

It's also possible that Larry created height in his younger brother. No one in the Jordan family is tall, and it looked as if fourteen-year-old Larry—who stood five feet seven inches—was always going to dominate his younger brother. But when Michael reached the ninth grade, he grew to five feet eight inches and, for the first time, could shoot over Larry. "After that, I never lost," Michael says. "Larry never grew past five feet ten inches and so he was in that five-feet-ten-and-under league. He was disappointed and angry and hurt."

From then on, the lazy boy who only worked hard at sports really dedicated himself to improving his basketball skills. On the ninth-grade team, Michael was the first to arrive at practice and the last to leave. At home, he practiced some more. And on weekends when no games were scheduled, he filled them with more practice.

It was lucky he had sports to burn off energy that year. He had watched "Roots" on television, and the spectacle of hundreds of years of racial injustice had sickened him. But instead of inspiring him to fight to overcome prejudice, "Roots" turned Michael into a rebel. He fought with his brothers and sisters, talked back to his parents, and quit a job as a maintenance man that his mother had forced him to accept. In school, when a white girl called him a name, he threw a drink in her face and got suspended. "I felt like a racist that year," he says.

Two things saved him: sports and his mother. Deloris Jordan isn't a woman you say no to, and when she ordered Michael to buckle down and do his homework, he shut up and did it. His grades improved and, as tenth grade started, so did his attitude.

Tenth grade was the first chance that students at Laney High School had to try out for varsity sports teams. Michael was five feet eleven inches then, and he thought he could hold his own against the school's best players. The varsity coach disagreed. He kept the only other sophomore who had tried out—Michael's six-foot-five-inch friend Leroy Smith—and banished Michael to the junior varsity. In public, Michael put on a brave front. At home, he wept.

But he didn't quit. Just the opposite—he worked harder. On the junior varsity team, he averaged twenty-eight points a game. That was enough, he thought, to get the attention of the varsity coach. He did, but not the way he wanted. The only reason he was invited to accompany the varsity to the regional play-offs was because the team's manager got sick and the coach needed someone to carry the uniforms and towels.

That year, though, a remarkable thing happened—Michael grew four and a half inches. This time, when he returned to school a junior, Michael easily made the varsity basketball team. The surprise was that he now began to work even harder. He practiced with the varsity and the junior varsity. He came to school early in the morning to shoot baskets before classes started. Every weekend, he could be found in the school gym.

Michael's hard work was even more important than his natural talent in attracting the attention of college coaches. Year after year, these coaches see high school players who are gifted athletes. But they know that many of those high school stars will never make a name for themselves in college because they rely too much on their talent. Michael Jordan, on the other hand, was not only gifted, he also had a great work ethic—he was always challenging himself.

The summer before his senior year in high school, Michael was invited to the Five-Star Basketball Camp in Pittsburgh, Pennsylvania. At this camp, older players and more experienced coaches taught some of America's best high school players. Just as important, the high school stars got a chance to compete against other gifted players their age. For Michael, this was an excellent opportunity to see how good he really was.

At this camp, he proved that he was just about the best high school player in America. In his first week, he won five trophies; the second week, he won five more. After that, colleges became even more interested in him.

One of those schools was UNC—the University of North Carolina. That pleased Michael's mother. She liked the North Carolina basketball coach, Dean Smith. Although he had never led a team to a national championship, he was known as a strict, wise, fair man with a genuine interest in his players.

Michael, however, was more interested in North Carolina State. Or in the Air Force Academy—he knew if he went there, he'd have a job after graduation. Mostly, though, he just hoped to go to college. "No one in my family had ever been, so I wanted to do that," he explains.

"And no one in Wilmington went to a Division I school, so I wanted to do that."

As Michael visited colleges, he kept coming back to the sterling reputation of Dean Smith. He was also continually reminded that UNC was sufficiently interested in its nonwhite students to sponsor Project Uplift, a special organization to help them. In the end, there was only one drawback to UNC—Dean Smith rarely put freshmen on his starting lineup. Michael considered that. And, deciding that was just another challenge, he chose the University of North Carolina.

In his first practice game at North Carolina in the fall of 1981, Michael Jordan flew over a seven-foot defender and made a spectacular dunk. Again and again, when he brought the ball upcourt, he drove to the basket without being stopped. "No one can guard him," Dean Smith said when he named Michael as one of his starting guards.

That was a rare honor, and Michael was humbled by it—but only off the court. In the gym, he began his career-long habit of "trash talking," that is, unnerving opponents by telling them he was going to make them look bad. In games, trash talking was a fact of life, a way of psychologically dominating opposing players. In practice, though, Michael's opponents were his teammates and friends. They didn't appreciate it when he'd dribble toward them and say, "I'm better than you, I can do this better than you."

Michael had a reason for bad-mouthing his teammates in practice—he wanted to make sure they were tough enough to rise to any challenge. His teammates didn't thank him for the lesson. Instead, they voted Michael the team's cockiest freshman and made him carry the film projector when they left Chapel Hill for games at other colleges.

"I love competition," Michael says. No matter how hard he played basketball, he never exhausted his need to compete. And so he would round up his friends for games of cards and pool. These contests sometimes lasted all night; Michael wouldn't let anyone quit until he had won.

Michael didn't put all of his efforts into competition— he had come to North Carolina for an education, and he was determined to get it. "Michael's first major was computer science," Deloris Jordan recalls. "He didn't know if he would make it as a professional." He worked hard in his courses and soon had a B average. His plan was clear: He would graduate, play professional basketball, and then become a teacher or work with comput-ers. There was nothing swelled-headed in that vision of the future.

But with Michael shooting consistently well, North Carolina won more games than it had in years, and in March of 1982, the team traveled to New Orleans,

Louisiana, to compete for the national college championship. The team continued to win. And on March 29, in front of more than sixty thousand people, Michael found himself playing against Georgetown for the college title.

Georgetown was a big, strong team led by Patrick Ewing, who was also a freshman. At seven feet one inch and two hundred pounds, Patrick was a powerful defender and a strong shooter. It was obvious even then that he would go on to greatness in professional basketball (and he has, as the captain of the New York Knicks). For North Carolina, the player to watch was not Michael Jordan but James Worthy, a sharpshooting forward who would become a star on the great Los Angeles Lakers team of the 1980s.

Few people expected that Michael Jordan—who had, just three years earlier, failed to make the varsity team in high school—would score the game's most important basket. But with half a minute to play and North Carolina losing by one point, Dean Smith called a time-out. "We can take one more shot," he told his players. "Get it to Mike."

Michael was too well guarded, so he passed the ball. His teammates whipped it around the court, returning it to him with just twenty seconds left on the game clock. There were two Georgetown players rushing toward him. Patrick Ewing was waiting to leap up and block the shot from behind. Michael didn't hesitate. From seventeen feet, he arched a rainbow so perfect that the ball barely stroked the cords of the net.

His two-pointer won the game—and made him famous. The telephone company in Chapel Hill, North Carolina, put a picture of "The Shot" on the cover of the phone book. Wilmington declared a "Michael Jordan Day."

The young man in the spotlight wasn't overly affected by all this attention. "It was the biggest shot of my life to that time," he says. "That's when Michael Jordan started getting his respect." Still, two days after the championship game, Michael was back in the University of North Carolina gym playing in a pickup game.

Michael polished his game in the gyms of Chapel Hill all that summer, and Dean Smith polished it some more that fall. The idea was to make Michael a complete player, as gifted on defense as he was on offense. But Smith was a strong advocate of team play, and as good as Michael was, it was important to Smith that he blend into the group.

Very quickly, North Carolina fans started telling a short, pointed joke: "Who's the only man who can hold Michael Jordan to twenty points a game? Dean Smith." The coach's disciplined approach worked. On the basis of his ballhandling as much as for his shooting, Michael was named to the all-American team and was honored by the

Sporting News as its College Basketball Player of the Year. In the summer of 1983, he starred on the American team that won a gold medal at the Pan American Games in Venezuela. And in his junior year at North Carolina, Michael was so dominant that he was asked to join the United States Olympic team.

Michael tried to keep his basketball excellence in perspective. When a photographer came to Chapel Hill to take his picture for the cover of *Sports Illustrated,* Michael insisted that he pose in a classroom. But it was increasingly difficult to keep his mind on the college experience—professional basketball teams were suggesting that he was, at twenty-one, ready to play in the pros.

The decision to leave North Carolina was a painful one. Deloris Jordan felt that he should stay in school: "I told him, 'No matter where you go and how much money you make, education will always win out. They can take your clothes, they can take your shoes, but they can't take what is inside your head.' " Dean Smith thought Michael had run out of challenges at the college level. And James Jordan wasn't sure if the same opportunity would be there for Michael at the end of his senior year.

Smith shared James Jordan's concerns. What if, Smith wondered, Michael didn't play as well in his fourth year? What if he got hurt? If he turned pro now, he would have a guaranteed contract that would make him and his family financially secure for a long time.

Michael thought about his decision for six long weeks. The night before he was supposed to make his decision public, he still didn't know how he felt. When he went to bed, he and his roommate were still debating the question.

The next morning, though, Michael Jordan knew what he had to do. "It's hard to give up part of your life, like your senior year in college," he said as he announced that he had indeed decided to play professional basketball. "But I have to do what's best for me." He had just made his first important business decision.

CHAPTER TWO

WHEN MICHAEL JORDAN turned pro, basketball was not the huge business it is now. On an average night, there were twelve thousand empty seats in Chicago Stadium, the home of the Bulls. Kareem Abdul-Jabbar, the center for the renowned Los Angeles Lakers, was the only player to earn $100,000 a year from a sneaker endorsement. Television rights for National Basketball Association games that cost a network $218 million for a multiyear contract in 1992 went for $20 million in 1979. The year Michael Jordan entered the NBA, Jerry Reinsdorf bought the Chicago Bulls for $16 million—the franchise is now worth at least $150 million.

The relatively modest numbers generated by professional basketball in the early 1980s are a reflection of the sport's low status at that time. There were few superstars.

Teams were generally unprofitable, with the typical franchise losing $700,000 a year. There was a leaguewide substance-abuse problem; in 1980, the *Los Angeles Times* estimated that between 40 and 70 percent of the NBA's players were using cocaine. Sneakers were the only part of a basketball player's uniform that allowed a star to express a personal preference, but the endorsement deals for sneakers weren't large. And there was a barrier that even marketing geniuses didn't know how to cross—how do you sell African-American basketball players to a nation accustomed to white sports heroes?

In 1984, Michael Jordan was only dimly aware of all this. "The first NBA game I ever saw was one I played in," he says. And his experience with the business of basketball was limited to making sure he got his share of the Adidas warm-up clothes that had been given to the North Carolina team.

So his hopes were modest. If an NBA team had offered him a contract with a salary of a few hundred thousand dollars a year and a signing bonus of a car, he would have been content. And if a shoe company had offered him an endorsement deal that would give him a little money, free warm-up clothes, and new shoes for every game, he would have been delighted.

Fortunately for Michael Jordan, he didn't have to arrange these contracts by himself. Dean Smith introduced him to

David Falk, a Washington lawyer who had been representing athletes since he graduated from law school in 1975. Most recently, Falk had negotiated the professional basketball contract for Michael's teammate at North Carolina, James Worthy. He thought Michael sounded "pretty marketable." That sounded about right to Michael, so he signed on with Falk.

Falk's first task was to negotiate a contract with the team that chose Michael. Players have no choice where they play—each year, the NBA holds a draft in the late spring in which teams get to pick college stars, with weak teams that haven't made the play-offs getting first pick. The college star who is the first player to be chosen often goes on to be a great star in the NBA. More immediately, that young man is often the NBA rookie who's offered the best endorsement deals.

Michael had twice been named College Basketball Player of the Year. While he was at North Carolina, the team had won eighty-eight games and lost just eleven times. When he left, he was already such a legend that the school retired his uniform number—twenty-three, which he had chosen because it was about half of forty-five, his brother Larry's number in high school. No one would have been surprised if Michael had been the first player chosen in the 1984 NBA draft.

Houston had the first pick, and the Rockets selected Hakeem Olajuwon, from the University of Houston, a towering center who had already made a name for himself. The Portland Trail Blazers chose next—and, instead of Michael, they picked Sam Bowie, who was also a center. So it was Chicago, with third pick, that got Michael.

In the early 1980s, the Chicago Bulls were a disaster. They had made the play-offs exactly once in the past seven years. In 1983–84, they had won twenty-seven games and lost fifty-five. While they were pleased to have a six-foot-six-inch guard with a great shot and a total commitment to winning, Michael wasn't really their first choice.

In fact, the men who ran the Bulls could barely conceal their distress at not getting Olajuwon. "We wish Michael were seven feet tall, but he isn't," the Bulls general manager said. "There just wasn't a center available. What can you do?"

There were, however, two good things about Michael's selection by the Bulls. One was that the team had no stars; he could make an impact there. The other was that Chicago was sports-crazy. If Michael played well and had an appealing personality, he would get a great deal of attention in the third-largest city in America.

The day after the NBA draft, David Falk got his first sense of Michael's charm and poise. He and Michael were flying to Chicago for the obligatory press conference, and he had written down a number of points he thought Michael ought to make. "I had barely gotten to my second point when Michael said, 'Thanks, I get the gist of what you're saying, I think I'll be able to handle it,' " Falk recalls. "Well, he sat down at a round conference table with all the microphones in front of him and about fifty people in the room. You could see from the very beginning this athlete was made for the media. He had a natural ability to communicate, to provide intelligent answers, to delicately handle the tough questions—he was incredible."

In 1983, Falk had engineered a $1.2 million deal for James Worthy that called for a sneaker company to name a shoe after him. This was a first. But there was a good business reason for it—the jogging boom was fading, the aerobics craze for women was peaking, and the sneaker companies needed something new to promote.

In Michael's final spring at North Carolina, Falk arranged for him to visit a number of shoe companies. At these meetings, Michael and his parents listened as executives told him all the benefits that would come Michael's way if he endorsed their product. Michael was unfailingly polite and attentive. But by the time he was scheduled to fly to Beaverton, Oregon, to visit Nike headquarters, he was sick of the process.

"I was tired of traveling," Michael says. "I had never worn Nike and I had never really liked Nike—I never wanted to go to the Nike meeting. I wanted to be with

Adidas, the company that had always given me clothes when I was at North Carolina."

Michael told his parents, "I'm tired of going back and forth. If Nike really wants to see me, let them come East." Deloris Jordan disagreed. "They can't make their full presentation if they have to come to you," she told her son. "You've got to go."

The Nike meeting was not just another presentation—the company had decided that Michael Jordan was too important for that. Nike had not come to this conclusion in the privacy of an executive conference room; no one there really knew Michael. But Sonny Vaccaro had seen Michael play. And Sonny Vaccaro was as good a basketball scout as Michael was a player.

Vaccaro had once been a promising athlete himself, but he chose to go to college rather than sign with the Pittsburgh Pirates. When he was twenty-four, he started a basketball tournament that featured America's best high school players. Later, he moved to Las Vegas and used his expertise for another purpose—in a city where gambling is the major business, professional gamblers asked him which football teams to bet on. In 1977, this unconventional expert became Nike's college basketball promotions representative. His assignment was to get the company's shoes on the feet of the country's best college players. A year later, ten of the best college basketball teams in the country were wearing Nikes.

Now Sonny Vaccaro was saying that he was willing to bet his job that Michael Jordan would be an American hero—and a terrific representative for Nike.

"My big thing was to find a gifted young athlete and market him," Vaccaro explains. "In the early 1980s, that person was Magic Johnson—Magic was Michael before there was a Michael. But Magic's representatives weren't up to making that happen. Then I watched Michael take that shot against Georgetown for all the money. And that told me he had the potential to transcend basketball. It wasn't just his ability—he had just the right body. Look at Shaquille O'Neal. You see seven feet two inches and three hundred pounds. No way can you stop him man-to-man. He's going to dunk in your face and break backboards for fifteen years. Doesn't matter. You can't be seven feet two inches and three hundred pounds. But you could be Michael—Michael didn't have an imposing body. He looked like anyone. And because he was like Mr. Person with these amazing abilities, I sensed that he could be a phenomenon."

And so Vaccaro told Nike, "You're prepared to sign endorsement deals with a few players for $200,000 each. Don't do that. Give all the money to one player. Give it to Michael Jordan."

As it happened, Nike had been considering Michael— as part of a group of endorsers that would include Charles Barkley and Patrick Ewing. But Rob Strasser, who was then head of marketing at Nike, was impressed by Vaccaro's argument. He made a video showing great moments of Michael's career with the Pointer Sisters singing "Jump" on the sound track. And he enlisted the support of Howard White, a former all-American from the University of Maryland who was Nike's link to African-American basketball players.

For all that, the Nike presentation didn't impress Michael. "Well, Howard was late, and they couldn't get the video going," Michael recalls. "I'm thinking: This is typical when you don't want to be somewhere, things start happening for the wrong reason. Eventually, they get through it. They say, 'What do you think about *that*?' I say, 'Great! Now can I go home?' "

Once he was back in North Carolina, however, Michael realized that the Nike offer was just too good to ignore—a shoe built just for him and his own line of clothing. In the negotiations with Falk, Nike had won very few points. If Michael failed to make the all-star team by the end of his first three years in the NBA, the company could discontinue his line of shoes. Or, if he made the all-star team but Nike didn't sell $3 million worth of shoes in any of those three years, it could also discontinue the line. But no matter what, Nike would have to pay Michael $250,000 a year for five years.

The length of that contract wasn't chosen haphazardly. "My parents and Coach Smith instilled business thinking in me," Michael explains. "I was about to make a lot of money, and I didn't know much about it. Without their guidance, I would probably have wasted the first two or three years. But my mother, she's all about, 'Maintain, keep what's yours, make sure no one takes advantage.' So equity was one of my first concerns when I hired David Falk. I told him, 'My first five years, I want to build a solid foundation. I don't want to take risks, I don't want to lay everything on the line. I want to build something solid, so that in the next five years, I can take more risks.'"

Armed with his newfound "business thinking," Michael went back to Adidas to see what the counteroffer might be. "I told them, 'I've always wanted to be with you. If you match this offer or just come close, I'll sign with Adidas.'" But Adidas couldn't match the Nike proposition. And so, reluctantly, Michael had to look hard at Nike. Beyond the money, there was an undeniable attraction: "an opportunity to have input on the shoe, to get a shoe I *like*." Viewed that way, there was no reason not to sign with Nike.

There was no time, that first year, to really design a special shoe for Jordan; the best Nike could do was slap new colors on an existing shoe. The designers chose red, white, and black, colors that made this particular sneaker look big and menacing.

The more difficult question, that first year, was how to

market this shoe in an exciting way. Initially, the line was simply going to be called "Michael Jordan." David Falk and Rob Strasser thought they could do better.

One afternoon, as they were brainstorming, Strasser told Falk about the new technology Nike was introducing in its track-and-field shoes. It gave runners a sense that they were running on air. That gave Falk an idea: "There it was, not 'Michael Jordan' but 'Air Jordan,' because it reflected the way he played."

Happily for Nike, Michael was named cocaptain of the United States team in the 1984 Olympics, which just happened to be played in Los Angeles. And there Michael put on a show that introduced the "air" player to every sports fan in that media-drenched city. In the first game, he scored fourteen points; in the second, he moved up to twenty. "Maybe we'll have a chance against the United States if we can put seven men on the court," the coach of the Uruguay team said before Michael's game. Playing with the standard five men, however, Uruguay was unable to stop Michael from scoring sixteen points. In the fourth game, he left the court at the foul line, floated toward the net, and finished his flight by spinning in midair and slamming down an over-the-shoulder dunk. "Michael's not human," the opposing coach said. "He's a rubber man."

Actually, he was a very dutiful son. The United States basketball team, as expected, won the gold medal. Although Michael was proud and excited, he didn't keep his. At the awards ceremony, with cameras recording every emotional moment, he called Deloris Jordan over and draped his medal around her neck. With that gesture, he became the darling of every mother in America—and made the Chicago Bulls and Nike very, very eager for the season to start.

CHAPTER THREE

S EE MICHAEL JORDAN in his first starring role since the Olympics," the Bulls proclaimed in the early fall of 1984. "Playing locally for forty-one nights only." Was Michael really that gifted? Was he worth the third-highest salary for a rookie in NBA history—$800,000 per year? Chicagoans came to find out. And even in exhibition games, Michael put on a show that energized his coaches and teammates as well as the fans.

The NBA did its part—it banned Michael's shoes. Too many colors, league officials said. If he's going to wear special shoes, they have to match the team's colors.

This ban was so helpful to Nike you have to wonder if it wasn't prearranged by the NBA and the shoe company. For Nike promptly made a new commercial: "On October 15, Nike created a revolutionary new basketball shoe. On

October 18, the NBA threw them out of the game. Fortunately, the NBA can't keep you from wearing them. Air Jordans."

On its heels, Nike created an even more powerful commercial. "Ready for takeoff," an announcer said over the sound of jet engines. And then, in slow motion, Michael glided across the screen, holding a basketball. As he approached the hoop, he thrust one arm behind him and opened his legs—he became "the Jump Man" that Nike would use as his personal insignia for the next decade. And then, as Michael dunked, an announcer asked, "Who said man was not meant to fly?"

That commercial made Michael as exciting as a rock star. He started off scoring huge numbers of points—thirty-seven and forty-five were not unusual for him that fall—and completely bewildering some of the league's most talented veterans with his astounding fakes. "There's no way to defend against him," player after player would complain. "You think he'll do one thing, then you think he'll do another, and in the end, he does something you've never seen before."

But then, everything about Michael was original. As he had at North Carolina, he wore uniform number twenty-three, but only the shirt was standard issue. He had his uniform shorts custom-made so they would be baggy and two inches longer than anyone else's. He wore a sweatband on his left arm and a knee protector just below his left knee.

For every game, he wore a brand-new pair of Nikes. He had to be the last Bull out of the locker room. And in Chicago Stadium, as he walked to the bench, he had to dust his hands with resin—for better ball control—and then clap them right in the face of the Bulls radio announcer.

Michael Jordan was, very clearly, having a terrific time.

There was nothing calculated about Michael; his exuberance was pure. He ate at McDonald's because he loved the burgers. When he made a television commercial for the Chevrolet dealers of Chicago and they offered him a car, he chose a practical four-wheel-drive Blazer instead of a flashy Corvette. Although he was making a huge salary, he was so unaffected that on Halloween, when a game took him away from home, he left an apologetic note on his door and invited trick-or-treaters to come back for goodies a few nights later. Most of all, he was so devoted to basketball that he'd say the game was "like a wife to me"—and he proved his devotion by forcing the Bulls to write a "love of the game" clause into his contract that allowed him to play pickup games in university gyms and school yards.

"Coming into the league, I was a naive kid," Michael says. "I didn't know the business around basketball. All I knew was, 'Let's play.' "

The people closest to Michael cherished his innocence and were intent on protecting it. "When Michael moved to Chicago, my stomach was in knots—here he was in a big city, and he didn't know a soul," his mother says. "So I came for the first three months, to help him set up. And for the first two years, he had a brother or sister there every other weekend."

Michael didn't need help avoiding the obvious pitfalls of sudden celebrity—new "friends" who just happened to deal drugs or have surefire business deals for him. His parents had taught him the dangers of drugs, and his business advisers had told him to refer all business propositions to them. But he had never been exposed to sophisticated big-city women, and it was hard for him to tell at first if they wanted to meet him because he was handsome, talented, and personable, or if their primary interest was his money.

Michael had only the briefest encounter with Robin Givens, a beautiful actress who was later to marry Mike Tyson, then the heavyweight boxing champion. "It lasted about a moment—that's all I needed to see that she and I weren't eye-to-eye," Michael says. But he was still very conscious of his social inexperience, so he came to rely more and more on the woman he knew best: "My mother became more or less my second eye. She can see a lot. The only person I totally trust is my mother—she brought me into this world, I have no reason not to trust her."

Over time, he came to be almost equally close to Howard White, who was just starting to run what's become known as "the Jordan desk" at Nike. "After Michael signed with us, I told him, 'Let me have a room in your house in Chicago, and everything will be fine,' " he explains. "I also went on the road with him."

Howard White was far more than a chaperone. "I was thirty-four, so Michael was like a younger brother to me," he explains. "With most women, if we met them, I'd be there after that. We'd sit down and play games with them—there was a lot of Truth or Dare. All those questions were on the table, and he'd get to learn a lot about these women."

As fame rolled his way, Michael became more inclined to let the world see that he was as open and amiable as he was talented. He wanted people to know that the star who could soar above the basket, tongue flapping, and score big points in every city with an NBA team was the same young man who would stand by the team bus, signing autographs and trading quips. It surprised no one that he was overwhelmingly elected to the Eastern Conference All-Star team—as a starting player who'd be taking the court alongside Larry Bird, Moses Malone, Julius Erving, and Isiah Thomas.

"I know I'll be so happy playing in that game," a thrilled Michael told reporters. "I'll be playing with four Hall of Famers who have already proven themselves. I'm going to be so nervous I probably won't remember how to play. I may not score a point."

He had that almost exactly right—the rookie who had burned up the league for months took only nine shots and scored just seven points in his first all-star game. But nervousness wasn't the only reason why. It's very possible that the ball was deliberately kept away from him because of resentment from the NBA's other star guards, Isiah Thomas and Magic Johnson. That, anyway, is what Magic Johnson's agent seemed to suggest after the game.

If players deliberately sabotaged Michael's all-star debut, their anger is understandable. Michael had come into the league with more bugles blowing than any rookie in history. He had played look-at-me basketball for months. And now, at the all-star game, he showed up for the slam dunk competition wearing gold chains and a red-and-black Nike sweat suit—while every other player wore his team's uniform. This attention-getting outfit wasn't a rookie mistake. It was part of Nike's marketing plan to show off its new line of Michael Jordan sports clothes.

"I was furious, disgusted, aggravated, and irritated," said the chairman of the NBA's marketing committee. "A league function shouldn't be used as a platform for advertising. I find it hard to believe that any players would try to freeze out another player. But when someone comes in there and obnoxiously pushes his own product like that—while everybody else is playing by the rules—you can't be sure."

Sonny Vaccaro defended the Nike move: "I liked it. We

created what we wanted to create. But maybe we used Michael."

As would often prove to be the case in Michael's career, only one opinion mattered—his own. And he was very, very hurt. As a younger player, he had admired Magic Johnson so much that he liked to be called "Little Magic." Now he was on notice: Some NBA stars he had idolized didn't wish him well.

How should he respond?

Michael decided to take his revenge on the court, at the very next game between the Bulls and Isiah Thomas's Detroit Pistons. Before the game, Isiah came over to Michael and apologized. Michael nodded. Then he went out and scored a breathtaking forty-nine points.

His advisers had to applaud that approach.

The all-star game freeze-out turned out to be a blessing for Michael. He had gone to the game wanting to be accepted by men he admired. He returned home knowing that he was not like them—and that he didn't want to be.

Rejection was, in his case, liberating. He got rid of the gold chains that a friend had described as a "Mr. T. starter set." In public, he took care to wear a white shirt, suspenders, suit, and tie—he was very conscious that he was becoming a role model, and he was determined to be a good one. And on the court, he gave up trying to fit in and concentrated on his single-minded obsession: winning.

The Bulls were not a winning team that year. But Michael was a winner. He scored 2,318 points—more than any player in the NBA, a very unusual achievement for a rookie. He pulled down 534 rebounds, more than any other Bull. To further establish himself as a gifted defensive player, he was responsible for 2.4 steals per game.

These impressive statistics meant a great deal to the Bulls. In Chicago, attendance soared 87 percent, with ticket sales almost doubling; on the road, more people came to see the Bulls than any other team. But for Michael, only one thing mattered—the team reached the play-offs, just as he had promised.

In postseason play, the Bulls were quickly eliminated. Michael played brilliantly—he always did when the games were important and the pressure was on. So it was as much in recognition of his effort as it was of his ability that he was named the 1984–85 NBA Rookie of the Year.

CHAPTER FOUR

IF MICHAEL JORDAN ever worried about Nike discontinuing his line because sales dipped below $3 million a year, he wasted his time. In his first year with the Bulls, Nike sold 2.3 million pairs of Air Jordans and another $18 million worth of his clothes. Total sales of Jordan products that year: $130 million. As one observer noted, if Air Jordan were a separate company, Michael would be head of the fifth-largest sneaker manufacturer in the world.

One thing about Michael Jordan—as good as he is, he always thinks he can do better. "I may have to score less and pass more this year," he told reporters at the start of his second season with the Bulls. "This is where I really have to concentrate this year, to step up and be a leader. I have the respect of all the players now, and if there are things that have to be said, I won't feel out of place."

At the start of Michael's second season, those words were prophetic. In the preseason, the Bulls had lost eight exhibition games and won none. A veteran player went to a drug treatment center. The Bulls released Michael's closest friend on the team. Then they made a trade that brought a new backcourt partner to Chicago: George Gervin, who had participated in the previous winter's freeze-out at the all-star game.

It certainly didn't look as if management was pampering its one superstar.

But the player who loved challenges rose to this one. In the first game of the season, he scored twenty-nine points and made the winning basket with twenty-three seconds left. In the second game, against the rough-and-ready Detroit Pistons, he was brutally fouled by the league's perennial bad boy, Bill Laimbeer. That led to a fight that got so out of control both coaches were ejected. Michael kept his cool; he scored thirty-three points to ensure the Bulls' victory.

But as the Bulls were on their way to their third straight victory, Michael suddenly dropped to the floor. That was not unusual. Players who dunk return to earth with a force six times their weight. Michael not only dunked, he flew to get there—and those acrobatic moves often ended with him sprawled on the court. He was so physically strong and mentally tough, however, that he always got up.

Not this time. Michael had to be carried from the court.

At first, the doctors thought he had suffered a jammed left ankle, so they taped him up and gave him crutches. Michael wasn't very concerned. "If I can walk without crutches, I'll try playing," he said. But when it was time for the next game, he was on the Bulls' bench, playing the unaccustomed role of cheerleader.

On November 5, 1985, Michael learned that the problem was much more serious than anyone had thought: He had a broken tarsal bone. Although it wasn't a dramatic fracture—even on an X ray, you couldn't see it—it had occurred in a bone that's slow to heal. The word was that Michael would be out of action for six weeks. "All I can think of is to lay up and do nothing," Michael said. "I don't know how to deal with it."

Another player might have dealt with this kind of injury by sitting on the Bulls' bench and supporting his teammates. But for all his talk about leading his team, Michael was unable to do that. Instead of joining the Bulls on their next road trip, he went back to North Carolina.

He said he was going to take courses at UNC and start collecting the handful of credits he needed in order to qualify for his degree. That was true. But it wasn't all he was doing in Chapel Hill. So Bulls executives had the dubious pleasure of turning on their television sets to watch a North Carolina basketball game—only to see Michael sitting on the bench next to Dean Smith!

That was too much to bear. Jerry Krause, the Bulls general manager, gently suggested to Michael that everyone would like him to join the team on the road trip. Michael refused. His reason, Michael said, was that he couldn't stand to see the Bulls lose. There was another reason—he'd started working out, hoping to add some bulk to his chest and arms, and he didn't want the team to know.

Michael's doctors planned to examine his foot in mid-December. If he was healing well, they were going to remove his cast. In that plan, Michael would return to the team in early January.

Hopes soared in Chicago, only to be dashed when the doctors announced that Michael would be out of action for at least another month. Michael was gloomy, but he cheered up in late December when he was sitting on the Bulls' bench before a game and a Bulls employee bet him ten dollars that he couldn't make a basket from that distance and that position. For the first time in weeks, Michael smiled. Then, on his second attempt, he put a perfect shot through the basket.

Michael's best present that Christmas was from his doctors—a lighter brace for his foot, an appointment for a checkup in mid-January, and a prediction that he'd be playing again on February 1. Once again, the doctors were too optimistic. In mid-January, when they examined Michael's foot, they discovered that it was still broken.

Michael couldn't stand it. He flew to see a doctor in Oregon for a second opinion. He flew to see a doctor in Cleveland for a third. No one told him what he wanted to hear.

Happily, the next examination revealed that the break was healing. Michael no longer needed the brace. Just a few weeks more, the doctors said—stay off your feet, you can rejoin the team in mid-February, right after the all-star game. Michael hated waiting. He knew it was irrational, but he would sit in his parents' home and will himself to heal faster.

Thinking he could cure himself by urging his body to heal was only one of the ways Michael was irrational that winter. He came to believe that the management of the Bulls really didn't want him to play again that season— and not because they were genuinely concerned about his foot. As Michael saw it, if he returned quickly to the team, he would lead Chicago to the play-offs. But he didn't believe that Reinsdorf and his aides wanted the team to do that well. He knew that if Chicago failed to make the play-offs, the Bulls would get a top-ranked college star in the NBA lottery. So maybe it wouldn't be so awful if the Bulls did poorly, didn't qualify for the play-offs, and then picked up that college star.

There is no evidence at all to suggest that Reinsdorf and his coaches really were that calculating. But there's plenty of evidence to show that Michael's fierce pride was pushing him to play as soon as possible. In fact, just as the sportswriters were starting to ask the inevitable question—Will Michael Jordan be out for the rest of the season?—Michael was deciding that he *had* to come back. In mid-February, he started playing in North Carolina. A little foul-shooting. Then some jump shots. Soon he was spending almost every afternoon in one pickup game or another. The fateful moment came when he dunked. He listened for the crackling of bones. There was nothing—he was ready to play professional basket-ball again.

The Bulls were not quite so delighted with this development. Very grudgingly, management allowed Michael to practice with the team—but first he had to submit to yet another round of doctors. And they found that there was still a small crack in the bone. If Michael played, he might reinjure his foot; if he rested, he'd be fine by the start of the new season.

Michael discussed the problem with Reinsdorf and Krause. Both men asked him not to play. Michael insisted. "A lot of people are saying I'd be a fool to come back," he told them. "They say I should come back next year. Well, they haven't experienced the game of basketball like I have. I wouldn't do anything to risk my career, but I think I can play. And I know I can make a decision that's best for Michael Jordan. So . . . you can either watch me play for the Bulls, or you can watch me play pickup games in

Chapel Hill. One way or another, I'm playing basketball."

What could Reinsdorf and Krause say to that? But in allowing Michael to rejoin the team, they insisted on a limit to his playing time—he would be allowed on the court just fourteen minutes per game, seven in each half. Michael was so excited to be wearing his Bulls uniform again that he didn't argue over the cap on his playing time. In the back of his mind, he really didn't believe Reinsdorf and Krause would enforce it.

On March 15, 1986, having missed sixty-four games, Michael returned to the Bulls. The crowd stood and cheered when he checked into the game—and went wild when he promptly dunked over the opponent's seven-foot-three-inch center. The coach kept a stopwatch on Michael, limiting him to thirteen minutes in regulation play. But the game ended in a tie, prompting an overtime period. Michael looked hard at the coach. The coach, however, never looked back. With Michael on the bench, the Bulls lost.

In his next game, Michael scored thirteen points in seven minutes; the Bulls lost. In his third game, Michael pushed the team ahead; when he left the court, the Bulls collapsed. "I'm hurting the team with these spurts," Michael concluded. "Either let me go back to playing a full game or forbid me from playing at all."

Again, management insisted on a compromise: twenty minutes of playing time a night, with two minutes added for every game. Michael's shooting became more consistent and he began to merge more with his teammates, but the Bulls continued to be an erratic team. Michael felt frustrated. If he played the whole game, he was sure the team would win consistently; at twenty minutes a night, however, there was only so much he could accomplish. He was, by now, convinced that Reinsdorf and Krause were deliberately sabotaging their team's chances.

So Michael forced a confrontation.

"I talked to my doctor today, and he told me the new X ray showed enough improvement that I could play the whole game," he told reporters. That's not exactly what the doctor had said. The doctor's point had been that although there had been no fresh damage to the bone, there hadn't been any new healing either: In his view, Michael shouldn't be playing basketball.

But Michael heard what he wanted. And what he heard made him lash out at the Bulls management: "It's not a medical decision anymore. It's a business decision. Just because you don't have a million dollars doesn't mean you go out and rob a bank. A lot of people make do with what they have—why can't we? Losing games on purpose reflects what kind of person you really are. If they really wanted to make the play-offs, I'd be in there whenever we had a chance to win."

Reinsdorf and Krause looked even worse in the Bulls' next game, when Michael's playing time expired with thirty-one seconds left in the game and the Bulls behind by one point. The coach took him out. Luckily, a great shot by John Paxson won the game for Chicago. But Michael was furious. "If I can play twenty-eight minutes, I can play another thirty-one seconds," he snapped.

The team's owner and general manager now looked petty and absurd. They insisted that avoiding the play-offs wasn't their intent, but Michael wouldn't be pacified. "I'm not a piece of property," he said. "I don't care what they pay me. I'm still a human being."

There was only one thing to do, and in mid-April, Jerry Reinsdorf did it—in the game that would decide whether Chicago made the play-offs, he let Michael play the entire forty-eight minutes. The Bulls won by two points. Michael's thirty-one points had made the difference.

The Bulls were now off to Boston and the play-offs.

No one expected the Bulls to beat Boston. The Celtics were the strongest team in the league, with a roster that included Larry Bird, Kevin McHale, Bill Walton, Robert Parish, and Danny Ainge. They were heavily favored to win the championship that year—and they eventually did.

First, though, they had to get through Michael.

Forget that Michael had played only eighteen games all season. Ignore the fact that his foot was, in his doctor's opinion, better off in street shoes than in Air Jordans. Consider only the psychology of a twenty-three-year-old who had won all his short life and who saw only winning ahead—this wasn't a player who was intimidated by the big bad Celtics.

"When I went to North Carolina, they all said I would sit on the bench," Michael told reporters as the play-offs began. "That was a challenge. This is similar. No one expects us to win, and we're going to take the challenge."

He meant exactly that. Although he was sick with a virus and had a headache, he sank his first five shots in the opening game. Sometimes all five Celtics converged on him as he moved into position to take a shot, but he still scored thirty points in the first half alone. His point total for that game: forty-one.

The Bulls lost, but the Celtics were awed. "Normally the guys on the bench are leaning forward, trying to make eye contact with me," the Celtics coach said. "When they saw what Michael was doing, nobody wanted to go in. I'd look down the bench, and they were all leaning back."

That spectacular performance was just a preview of the athletic genius Michael displayed in the second game of the play-off series. This time, Boston had prepared special defenses for him. But Michael was in what's known as a "zone"—nothing could stop him. "He was so quick that if he had just slowed to a blur we might have had a chance," a Boston player said afterward.

Michael scored and scored, single-handedly keeping Chicago in the game. And he almost won it all by himself—with nine seconds to play and Chicago down by two points, he stole the ball and took a three-point shot. He was crushed when it bounced off the rim, then elated when the referee called a foul. Michael had two shots. With the Boston fans roaring for him to miss, he coolly sank both shots, forcing an overtime period.

As the clock ticked off the final seconds of that overtime, Michael took a desperation shot that missed. The game was still tied. Now there would have to be a second overtime. Once again, Michael reached deep inside himself for a superhuman effort. It wasn't enough. Boston won, 135-131.

For most everyone who saw that game, the outcome was dwarfed by Michael's remarkable sixty-three points, a play-off scoring record that still stands. "He is the most awesome player in the NBA, and he put on one of the greatest shows of all time," Larry Bird said.

"I just wish I could have been a spectator—being on the court with him, you could tell something magical was happening," Orlando Woolridge added.

Only one person was critical of Michael's play that day, and that was Michael. He didn't particularly care about the sixty-three points. His concern was winning. And when he had a chance to achieve that—at the end of the first overtime—he failed. "I can't believe I missed that last shot," he told reporters.

The Celtics went on to sweep the series, and the Bulls went home for the summer. But Michael had not only regained his form, he had surpassed himself. The future looked as bright and open as his famous smile.

CHAPTER FIVE

THE IDEA WAS for Michael to sign autographs for his young fans at a mall in Dallas, Texas. The sponsors of the event knew that Michael had many admirers, so they hired security guards and arranged for Michael to stay for ninety minutes. That was, they thought, plenty of time for Michael to sign every card and shake every hand.

"It was *crazy*," Michael recalls, scowling at the memory of that disastrous day. "I had a tiny table and four security guards—just four—with five thousand people in line. And everybody was pushing. Little kids were up front, which I love, because I wanted to do it for the kids, but it became a bad scene. There was a practice or film session or something I needed to be at, and I had to leave before I'd signed for everybody. Well, the crowd started circling. The guards had to get around me and push through all those people. Everybody was shoving pens at me—I was getting stuck in the side, in the face. It was *scary*."

Michael reluctantly drew the obvious conclusion: no more autograph signings, many fewer public appearances. "I have a tough time saying no, but it's just not worth it. You're not going to be able to sign for everybody or satisfy everybody, and when you don't, they get mad at you."

Michael was just beginning to discover the high cost of fame.

Celebrity has always required a trade-off. The famous get admiration, wealth, and privilege; they give up a certain degree of privacy. In the past, that trade-off wasn't particularly bothersome. Movie stars had press agents who spooned inoffensive stories to grateful reporters. Musicians and authors were interviewed mostly about their work. And sports stars were considered fit only to discuss the finer points of their particular expertise.

As Michael Jordan was growing up, all that changed. In the early 1970s, there was a tremendous interest in hard news, as investigative journalists focused on what first seemed like an unimportant burglary at the Watergate apartment building in Washington, D.C. But that burglary was only the tip of a scandal that led directly to President Richard Nixon. What those journalists learned eventually forced the president to resign—the first time that had ever happened.

But journalists were not heroes for long. In the late 1970s, the American people were preoccupied with their own problems as the economy stumbled and millions of people lost their jobs. The public wanted a rest from serious subjects. In 1980, with the election of Ronald Reagan, they got their wish. They wanted prosperity and tranquility, not controversy and complication. Reagan gave them all that.

Now the press had good news to celebrate. People who weren't prospering were ignored, while those who were getting and spending became overnight celebrities. In the absence of more meaningful role models, traditional celebrities—actors, musicians, athletes—became like gods and goddesses. The vast machinery of the media seemed to be dedicated to providing readers and viewers with every last scrap of information about these people.

No group was more lionized during this period than athletes. They seemed purer and more heroic than other celebrities—unlike other performers, they worked without scripts. Their feats required not just great bodies but years of training, quick thinking, and, often, a fair amount of courage; watching athletes play, you could get a sense of their character as well as of their skills.

As a sport, basketball was ideally suited to turn its

stars into celebrities. There are only five players on the court, and they are, for the most part, articulate young men who have been college educated and exposed to the media. Basketball is simple to follow, and the ball is easy to see. The court is small enough so everyone in the stadium can get a fair view of the players' faces, something that can't be said about football or baseball. The ball is constantly in play and points mount up quickly, making basketball a livelier game than baseball or football. And, most important of all, basketball is the one team sport that can be dominated by one dazzlingly gifted player.

In the early 1980s, that player was Magic Johnson. But Magic chose Charles Tucker, who was his godfather and was based in Detroit, to be his agent. Tucker meant well, but he was unable to develop connections with big companies. And although Magic played in Los Angeles—the most significant media city west of the Mississippi—Tucker was also unable to shake the advertising community's long-held belief that black stars couldn't effectively sell products to white consumers.

Then came Michael Jordan.

"I have a romantic view of Michael," said Rob Strasser, who had championed his signing at Nike. "More than any athlete I've ever seen, he can put chills up my spine on a regular basis." Nike capitalized on that idea in Michael's rookie season. "The theme was Air: an athlete in a glorious achievement," explains Jim Riswold, the creative director of the advertising agency that has handled the Nike account for most of Michael's career.

The strategy worked. People noticed Michael's genius first, his race second. Or maybe they didn't even notice his race. "Is Michael black?" asks Bulls owner Jerry Reinsdorf, not entirely in jest. "Michael has *no* color—he's transcended it."

Other shoe companies had to learn the hard way that Michael's blend of innocence, enthusiasm, and great showmanship was unique. The year after Air Jordans hit the market, there were nine basketball shoes with the names of star players on them. Every last one of them flopped.

In 1986, Nike decided that it was time to take Michael to the next level—to remove him from the pedestal that the company had put him on and show him as a person. To do that, they hired Riswold, whose advertising agency, Weiden and Kennedy, was based in Portland, Oregon, just a few miles from Nike headquarters. Riswold had once worked for a professional basketball team, and he knew how critical sports stars could be of one another. So he was extremely impressed by the praise for Michael that came from Boston Celtics legendary center Bill Russell: "Michael is a better person than he is a basketball player."

To make commercials that would illustrate this idea,

Riswold turned to Spike Lee, a New York filmmaker who had never made a commercial. But he had recently written and directed a feature film called *She's Gotta Have It*. In that movie, he also acted, playing a character named Mars Bonfire, who was such a big fan of Michael's that he wore his Air Jordans everywhere. That gave Riswold an idea. Mars Bonfire came from Brooklyn, and his attitude was gritty, urban, and irreverent—if Spike Lee played Mars in the commercials as well, he would be an ideal partner for Michael.

The "Spike-and-Mike" commercials made Michael as hip as he was wholesome. They showed him talking and joking, so he looked witty and intelligent. They connected him both to the suburban white audience and to urban blacks. They established him as a man with a smile as big as his talent, encouraging female viewers to regard him as adorable rather than threatening. They made him, in short, a celebrity endorser with many positive characteristics and not a single negative one.

Other companies noticed, and many more endorsement opportunities followed. Michael welcomed these opportunities. What he didn't welcome was the loss of his freedom that came along with them. In 1986 and 1987, however, he still liked to think he could be both a regular guy and a colossal star. And so, every time his fans pestered him for autographs in restaurants or cornered him in a store, he was at once pleased and annoyed.

*   *   *

When Michael was deciding if he ought to leave the University of North Carolina or stay for his senior year, he took refuge on the golf course. There he was far removed from fawning admirers, would-be business partners, and all the other people who wanted a piece of him. Alone on the golf course, he could think.

In the summer after his second season, Michael began playing golf every day. And not just one leisurely round. He'd play thirty-six holes, moving at top speed. Sometimes he'd play with friends like Charles Barkley. But he was just as comfortable playing alone.

"I don't need an opponent to be competitive," he explains. "The course is going to shoot seventy-two every time I face it—that's a consistent opponent. For a guy who feels he has to win every day, that's enough to drive me. I feel it will replace basketball for me. I love it so much. It's time-consuming. And it's impossible—you can't conquer it."

A brisk thirty-six holes will work up a sweat, but no one would call that a full workout. And yet, when the Bulls' doctors examined Michael after that summer and tested his body fat, they were stunned. About 8 percent of an Olympic athlete's weight will be fat—Michael's body was just 3 percent fat!

Clearly, the young man who saw nothing wrong with

a diet of fast-food hamburgers knew himself fairly well. His foot was completely healed. He was, more than ever, ready to play. And now he was even more committed to winning.

In the first game of the 1986–87 season, Michael scored fifty points to lead the Bulls to victory. That game was a forecast of his year. In that season, Michael scored 3,041 points, making him only the second player in NBA history—Wilt Chamberlain was the first—to break the 3,000-point barrier. But on the day he scored sixty-one points to establish that record, the Bulls lost. "I know records are meant to be broken, and I know I am the only guard in the history of basketball to have scored this many points," he said. "But these records and marks meant nothing. I would rather have had the win, because that would have clinched the seventh play-off spot in the Eastern Conference."

Michael had to deal with a massive amount of personal bests that year. He scored forty points or more in nine consecutive games and twice scored more than sixty; in one game, he broke an NBA record by scoring twenty-three consecutive points without a miss. His average of 37.1 points was good enough to earn him the first of seven straight NBA scoring titles.

As brilliant as those offensive figures are, Michael was

just as dominant as a defender. That year, he blocked 125 shots and made 236 steals, making him the only player in NBA history to block more than 100 shots and record more than 200 steals in a single season.

Yet the achievement that people remember best from that season didn't take place in a game. It was in the Seattle Kingdome, at the slam dunk competition before the all-star game. This time, Michael wore his Bulls uniform and that year's Air Jordans, which were a pristine white. And this time, Michael put on a show that no one could criticize.

He started at half-court and then, step by step, moved back, like a pilot who knew his jet needed an extra-long runway. Head down, he dribbled upcourt, gathering speed. Liftoff occurred at the foul line. Time slowed as he floated toward the basket, his eyes glued to the rim, his expression fierce as a warrior's, his tongue flapping, the ball cradled in his right hand. He seemed to descend, then level off, then—incredibly—rise again. And then, high above the basket, he slammed the ball through the net in an explosion of energy that had everyone screaming.

And that was only one of his dunks.

Michael showed the range of his repertoire that night. Once he changed course in midflight, swinging around the rim in midair. Another time, he held the ball low in both hands. For his final dunk, he approached the basket from the left, flicked the ball into his right hand, and hooked the ball into the basket almost as an afterthought.

Michael usually chalks up such performances to instinct and intuition. "I don't plan—you *can't* plan," he says. "It just happens. What looks unique is instinct. It's what I've done all my life." This time, though, even he was amazed: "When I look back on that dunking contest, it's just unbelievable that I was able to do those things."

It was a foregone conclusion, after that performance, that Michael would win the slam dunk competition. When he did, he accepted the $12,500 cash prize. But he didn't keep the money—he shared it with his teammates, giving $1,000 each to eleven Bulls.

Although victory in the slam dunk competition and a handful of personal awards were pleasing to Michael, he was still unsatisfied at the end of the season. Once again, the Bulls made the play-offs, and, once again, they were quickly eliminated by the Celtics.

It did matter to Michael that he played well, but his dominance was, by now, becoming a double-edged sword. The better he was as an individual star, the more he was open to criticism as an "incomplete" player who couldn't function efficiently with the other players on his team. So what if he was the league's most thrilling and accomplished scorer and its most devastating defender? One man can't win a championship by himself. For the first time, people were joking about "Team Jordan"—a description of the Bulls that would intensify until they were routinely called "Michael Jordan and the Jordanaires."

Michael seethed. This charge diminished his stature, making him appear more selfish and less effective than the league's star playmakers, Larry Bird and Magic Johnson. But he didn't think he was the problem. And he said so: "My teammates have a tendency to stand around and let me do everything. I get disappointed that they aren't respected, yet they don't respond."

It was strange. As Michael's personal achievements mounted, the prize he sought more than any other seemed further and further away.

There was one victory that Michael scored in his third season that didn't involve his team, or even his celebrity. It was in his personal relations. And almost the best part of his fortuitous meeting with Juanita Vanoy was that he noticed her first.

Juanita wasn't like the women who would sometimes lie down in front of his car in order to meet him, or who sent him suggestive pictures of themselves with their phone numbers scribbled on the back. She was a banking executive. She was a few years older than he was. And although she had certainly heard of Michael, she was mature enough to know that a relationship only works when the people involved genuinely care for each other.

"When Michael told me he'd met this woman and that

she was really nice, signal lights went on," Howard White recalls. "Michael and I would make dinner for her and one of her girlfriends at his place. Or we'd go to the movies. I could tell that he was taken by her."

For all that, Michael was not ready to settle down with anyone. In high school and college, he dated so little that he had almost come to believe he would be a bachelor all his life. He cooked and cleaned for himself—he even sewed—so he wasn't looking for a woman to take care of him. And he was only twenty-three years old, traveling all the time, and loving it.

"Sometimes my best friends—my boys—fly in," he has recalled, his eyes flashing as he remembers all those visits in NBA cities. "We sit in the room and never leave. I think that's great. I love that. It's like college. I missed my senior year, so I think, Michael, this is your senior year. We talk, we play cards—I think that's great, I love it. I get myself ready for the game."

The fact is, Michael explains, he loves playing in other cities: "I like it almost better than playing at home. You've got a challenge staring you dead in the face—the crowd's greatest expectation is that I'll score fifty points and we'll lose. Someone else's home court; yes, I *like* that."

Howard White took Juanita aside to tell her that Michael was still more taken with marathon card games and good times with his childhood friends and, most of all, basketball, than he was with the idea of settling down. But, he emphasized, she shouldn't despair. "I told her, 'It isn't right now, but when he's ready, you'll be the person—that I know,' " Howard says. "There were enough cutout points that if he wanted it to be over, she would have been gone."

So maybe the 1986–87 season wasn't so bad after all.

CHAPTER SIX

THE SCORE in the practice game was 4-4. Or was it 4-3? Michael was sure the game was tied. Doug Collins, the Bulls coach, insisted that Michael's squad was losing. He knew that Michael competed so intensely in practice that some of the players assigned to guard him burned out and had to leave the team, so he expected that Michael would respond to the challenge. Instead, Michael stalked off the court.

Still steaming, Michael took the dispute public. "I'm a competitor, I want to win—and I *always* keep score," he told reporters. "After a long, tough practice, the losing team has to run laps. I felt that Coach Collins was stacking the odds against me on purpose. If he wants me to run, fine—stop practice and I'll run all he wants. But why make me kill myself in the scrimmage and then make me run?

People may say this is trivial. When you're a competitor and you want to win, nothing is trivial."

Two days later, Michael and his coach made peace. But the event was a signal: Michael's commitment to winning had become a virtual fever. "I *despise* losing, and I would do anything to avoid it," he says. "I never feel I've lost until the game is over."

In past years, Michael had become used to bearing almost total responsibility for the fate of games. Everyone knew that at the end of a close game, he was going to be the Bull with the ball. "I love when it comes down to that one moment and it's all in my hands," he explained. "No matter what the game is or who you're playing against, you have to want the ball. The clock, the pressure—you block all that out. All you think about is what you have to do to win."

In 1987, though, the Bulls management had finally assembled a group of players who seemed compatible with Michael. They couldn't play at his level, of course. But they were, physically and temperamentally, well suited to set aside their own dreams of stardom in order to help their team.

Charles Oakley was back, just as solid as ever; he was a prodigious rebounder and enforcer who wasn't afraid to dive for balls and rumble under the basket. John Paxson was becoming an even more deadly three-point shooter, capable of swishing long shots with the kind of confidence most players only have about layups. The team's hopes for improvement, though, rested on two young players, Scottie Pippen and Horace Grant. Scottie was fast, fearless, and a great shooter; Horace was muscular and aggressive, a good offensive complement to Charles Oakley. At last, Michael felt, the Bulls had a chance to get beyond the first round of the play-offs.

But the Bulls' beauty was only skin-deep. As the season wore on, it was once again clear that the Bulls and Michael Jordan were generally synonymous. If Michael had a little support, the Bulls won. If he was seriously challenged or had an off night, the Bulls lost.

Michael was hot much more often than not that year. By midseason, his personal statistics were so uniformly outstanding that more fans voted for him for the all-star team than any other player. At that game, Isiah Thomas— who had been one of the players who embarrassed Michael in his first all-star outing—was so eager to make things right that, the joke went, he passed the ball to Michael even when Michael was sitting on the bench. With that kind of help, Michael scored forty points and was named the game's Most Valuable Player.

Not long after that, Jerry Reinsdorf decided that Michael was seriously underpaid. There was no reason for him to do anything about that—Michael's contract still had more than a year to run. But as Reinsdorf knew, every home game since November of 1987 had been a sellout; as a waiting list for tickets began to grow, it was clear that there wouldn't be an empty seat in Chicago Stadium as long as Michael played there. CBS/Fox was making a video called *Higher Ground*, its first-ever Bulls diary. And merchandise with the Chicago logo was becoming a big seller, bringing still more revenue and recognition to the team.

Like all owners of NBA teams, Reinsdorf had a salary cap—a league-imposed limit on what he could spend on his payroll. But he wanted Michael to know how much he was appreciated. And because money is the form that appreciation takes in such matters, he wanted Michael to be the highest-paid player on any professional sports team. So without any prompting from Michael, Reinsdorf met with David Falk and hammered out a new contract that quadrupled Michael's salary and, for a while, made him the best-paid player in the league.

Now Michael would get $25 million for eight years, or $3.125 million a year—more than $30,000 per game. That is a great deal of money. But then, Michael was about to be named the league's Most Valuable Player. He was also the NBA's Defensive Player of the Year. A computer couldn't have designed a more complete basketball player: Michael was the first player in the history of the NBA to have the best statistics in both scoring (2,868 points, an average of 35 per game) and steals (259 for the season). And, most important to Michael, he led his team to the play-offs.

Michael was getting tired of playing hard all year, winning a slot in the play-offs, and then seeing the Bulls eliminated in the first round. In the spring of 1988, the Bulls were starting out against the Cleveland Cavaliers. This time, Michael decided he would so dominate the opening game that Cleveland couldn't recover.

Scoring fifty points certainly sent that message and assured the Bulls' victory in the first game. That was just the prelude. In game two, Michael scored fifty-five points— the first time any NBA player scored fifty points in consecutive games. The Bulls won again. One more victory, and Cleveland would be history. But the Cavs didn't cave in. In game three, they held Michael to what, for him, was a shutout—a mere twenty-eight points, not enough to save the game for the Bulls. Michael rallied in game four, scoring forty-four points, but Cleveland won again.

Now the series was tied. But could Michael keep up his torrid pace? Would he have to keep on scoring half of the Bulls' points? Or would his teammates finally step up?

The important statistic in game five wasn't that Michael scored thirty-nine points but that Scottie Pippen added twenty-four more and made some breathtaking defensive plays. For once, Michael wasn't a one-man team. And for once, the Bulls won a play-off series and were bound for Detroit.

Every team has its own identity and style of play. For the Detroit Pistons in the late 1980s, that style was politely called "physical." More typically, it was labeled "dirty"— a Pistons game seemed to have more than the usual amount of violent fouls, bloody noses, and flying bodies. But this style worked well for Detroit; because opposing players were fearful of getting hurt, the Pistons won the all-important "head game" that makes the difference in contests between teams that are otherwise equally talented.

A month before the play-offs began, Michael played one of his best games ever, scoring fifty-nine points against the Pistons. Chuck Daly, Detroit's coach, was determined that wouldn't happen again. And so he and his assistants devised a special defense that would, they believed, shut down Michael's awesome offensive attack. They called it "the Jordan Rules."

The Jordan Rules weren't that original. Other teams had tried defenses with the same aim—to keep Michael from the basket and force him to take long shots. Their method, however, was simply to defend the basket with a wall of bodies. The Pistons' plan was more clever. Under the Jordan Rules, there was no wall of bodies. Michael was, therefore, encouraged to drive into the lane. But as soon as he got the ball and started moving toward the basket, two or three defenders cut over to block the lane, with another slicing across to greet him on the way. If Michael had a teammate set a pick for him, a Piston would rush between Michael and his blocker. And if Michael chose to go to the air, there was every likelihood he would be rewarded with elbows to the body and hands in his face. He might get his points, but he'd have to pay the price. Eventually, the Pistons hoped, he'd get tired and have to pass to his less talented teammates.

This plan worked well in the first game of the series. Michael scored twenty-nine points—for him, a lackluster game—and Detroit won by eleven. In the second game, though, Michael stormed back with thirty-six points, and the victory went to Chicago. That enraged the Pistons.

They took action quickly and dramatically. At the very start of the third game, Pistons bad boy Bill Laimbeer came up on Michael's blind side and launched an elbow right into his stomach. That foul produced another one, as Michael lunged at Laimbeer. And Michael's frustration was just beginning. Detroit players hounded him as if he were the only Bull on the court; after seventeen minutes, Michael didn't have a single point. At game's end, Michael had managed to score thirty-one points. It wasn't enough. The Pistons now led 2-1. After that, the Pistons ruled, winning two games in a row to eliminate the Bulls.

It had been a great year for Number Twenty-three. But expectations were now so high for Michael that his excellence was starting to be held against him. "Teams with scoring champions don't win championships," fans were saying. The more Michael proved his greatness, the more it seemed that the ultimate prize was eluding him. Now, in his sights, he saw just one target: the NBA championship.

CHAPTER SEVEN

THINK ABOUT how many kids would love to be professional basketball players—*millions* of kids," Michael says. "To see those odds, to know that one out of 200,000 kids makes it, and then to have that chance . . . in this time when jobs are hard to come by and you look at this game and the money we make, well, you can't ask for a better position. To play a game and get paid, that's the easiest job in America—and to play for two hours and earn an average salary of $1.1 million, that is *amazing*."

That's seeing the bright side. There's another, and in that way of looking at stardom, the professional athlete gives something back for everything he or she gets. This other reality was very much on Michael's mind in 1988— the first year in which the business of Michael Jordan eclipsed both his achievements on the basketball court and the pleasure he took there.

"Business is also a game," he said early in 1993, having resigned himself—temporarily, it turned out—to stardom's strange balance of rewards and annoyances. In 1988, though, he didn't have that emotional balance. He was being pulled in different directions in his business dealings; only on the basketball court could he find peace.

He had, for example, signed endorsement contracts that he and his advisers had intended to protect him completely—only to discover the NBA had retained some marketing rights and was exploiting them in ways he thought were inappropriate. He had agreed to make himself available for commercials and photo sessions, only to learn they could eat up all of his free time. And when an opportunity arose to be part of an exciting new business, he found himself in a war with his present partners.

And then there were situations that troubled him on a more daily basis. He was having problems with the Bulls coach. He didn't approve of some personnel changes. Juanita was pregnant, a condition that often prompts reluctant men to get married, but he still wasn't sure if he was ready for marriage.

The last thing Michael wanted, in 1988, was conflict in his life. Other men—even other stars—might put up with aggravation, or ignore it, or look for ways to postpone dealing with it. Not Michael. For this twenty-five-year-old, problems were to be confronted and solved.

Controlling the length of photo sessions and commercial shoots was simple. Michael just announced he was going to leave at a certain point. And then he did.

"My mind is fixed when I go in to do these things," he explains. "It's just like, in a game, I know I have forty-eight minutes. So when I go into a commercial and they say, 'We have four hours today and six hours tomorrow,' I'll say, 'No, we don't need that much time. I'm a professional. We won't need all those takes and retakes. You don't get five free throws when you're fouled; you get two and that's it.' I've never gotten angry about it. I've always stretched myself. I don't want to embarrass Nike—I represent them—so I don't walk off the set if they're not quite finished."

One time, though, for another company, Michael had to draw the line. "It was a four-hour shoot, and the director wasn't quite organized," he recalls. "The shots took longer and longer, and, next thing you know, I'd been there five and a half hours. I was really steaming. I felt they were taking advantage of my niceness. I'd told them I had another appearance right after the shoot—which I did—and finally I just said, 'I'm sorry, but I gotta go.' First time I ever walked out. Later, I looked at the commercial—it's a great commercial! Ever since then, they send someone who really knows me onto the set to speed it up."

In his dealings with Nike, Michael had just the opposite problem—life was moving too fast. He had been extremely happy working with Rob Strasser and Peter Moore, the company's advertising expert, but as 1987 ended, they left Nike. His only real links to the company now were with Sonny Vaccaro, who was a scout, and Howard White, who was more of an adviser than a decision maker. As for Phil Knight, Nike's founder and president, Michael hardly knew him.

What made Michael's lack of relationships at Nike suddenly important was that his Nike contract was coming up for renewal. It was certain that Nike wanted him to stay, and that the new contract would be extremely lucrative. The question was, who would he work with at Nike after the deal was done?

Moore and Strasser weren't making matters any easier for Michael. They had what seemed like a great idea for him—he would continue to wear and endorse Nike shoes, but he'd join them in the creation of a company that would design and market sports clothes. They intended to call it Michael Jordan, Inc.

"We did an imaginary annual report for Michael Jordan, Inc., for the year 2000," Strasser recalled in 1992. "We saw this as a company that would break new ground. We thought Michael could be the black Ralph Lauren."

"What we had learned—and Michael had learned—was how to market a superstar celebrity," Moore added. "We hoped to take Michael way beyond sports, beyond shoes and clothes, into cosmetics and cologne. And we didn't think Michael needed to play forever in order for the company to succeed. 'Just win one championship and play until 1991 or 1992,' we told him. 'After that, it's okay to run your car into a ditch.' "

Michael was intrigued. Nike would lose nothing, and he would gain something. So, with Moore and Strasser in tow, he went to see Phil Knight.

This meeting was a disaster. "That's not possible—we're not going to do that," Knight said, according to a book about Nike called *Swoosh,* which was coauthored by Strasser's wife, Julie. "Michael Jordan without Nike won't mean anything."

After that, Michael's father said, "he was torn." On one hand, Michael's ownership share in a new company could have produced much more money for him than anything Nike was offering. "But it would take four or five years to get started," Michael realized, "and if anything happened to me, the damage would be to the company."

Slowly he realized that he didn't have to make these negotiations into a battle. If anything, Strasser and Moore had presented him with a magnificent gift, a leverage point, a negotiating tool—he could use their offer to get a better deal from Nike. And that's just what happened. As the talks continued, the Nike deal got richer. Finally Nike's offer reached $20 million, and Michael decided it was time to talk it over with Rob Strasser.

"When Rob found out what Nike was offering," Michael says, "he asked me *not* to go with Peter and him. He said I should go Nike's way." And so Michael signed his second contract with Nike, one that would last to the year 2000—beyond his playing career.

That contract reflected Michael's enormous contribution to Nike. In 1984, the company's sales were $850 million; by 1988, it was riding a growth curve. Its advertising had been crucial in that growth, and Michael had been crucial to that advertising. Now everybody knew that Nike was about more than running shoes.

With Michael's future at Nike assured, Phil Knight thought it was time to turn the company into a national—and then global—institution. That meant more television advertising. And that meant a much bigger role for Michael. "You can't explain much in sixty seconds," Knight concluded, "but when you show Michael, you don't have to."

In November of 1988, Michael became the father of Jeffrey Michael Jordan. The birth of his first child was his only clear-cut pleasure that fall. Off the court, the Bulls had made a trade that seemed worse than counterproductive—it was like a slap in his face.

The trade had been engineered in the off-season, when Michael was off playing golf. In that exchange, the Bulls had sent Charles Oakley to New York, and New York had sent the Bulls a veteran center named Bill Cartwright. Michael was furious. Oakley was, in his opinion, the best rebounder in the NBA—and he was Michael's only real friend on the team. Cartwright, though talented, was slow, aging, and somewhat clumsy. Chicago may have needed a center, but Michael didn't see how this one was going to help him lead the Bulls to a championship.

Michael had it right. He was playing almost every minute of every game, but after twenty games, the Bulls had won ten and lost ten. This was the worst start since he'd joined the Bulls.

When a team with the greatest player in the league is in a slump, people point fingers and assign blame. Michael didn't. The Bulls general manager did. And he thought the reason for the team's slow start was Michael Jordan, whose high salary kept the team from buying some other expensive talent and whose insistence on taking every important shot crippled his teammates.

The team seemed to jell in midseason. But that was a fluke. The Bulls had a pattern: Win a few and then collapse. In desperation, Michael met with Coach Collins to formulate a strategy to hold the team together. Their conversation was cordial, but over the next few games, it became clear that Michael had made his own decision about the new tactics that were necessary—and he had decided that he would be more effective as a point guard than as a pure shooter.

Now he made fewer crowd-pleasing dunks. Instead, he passed more often to his teammates. This heightened emphasis on the four other Bulls on the court challenged them—and transformed them. Chicago started winning regularly. Then came a plague of injuries. The Bulls might be going to the play-offs, but they would be limping in.

The Cleveland Cavaliers were heavily favored to whip the Bulls—even to sweep the series. Michael was unfazed. He grandly predicted that his team would win. And then he set out to prove he was a prophet.

After three games, the score was 2-1 in the Bulls' favor. If Chicago won the fourth game, it would very likely take the series; if Cleveland won it, the series would be tied and the Cavs would enjoy a psychological edge. So both teams approached game four as if it were the championship itself.

The tension didn't hit Michael until the end of the fourth quarter, with less than a minute to play. The score was tied. And he had just been fouled. This was a scenario made for Michael. But he made only one of his two shots.

With just seconds to go, the Bulls held a one-point lead. Again, Michael was fouled. And again, he made only one of his two shots.

And, as drama would have it, Cleveland tied the game at the buzzer. In the overtime period, an exhausted Michael Jordan had nothing more to give. Cleveland won by three points to tie the series.

Howard White spent that evening with Michael, watching him stare at a blank TV screen. He understood why. "With superstars, it's almost like a religion—they don't believe they can lose," he says. "When Michael doesn't win, it's like a travesty for him. He just can't believe it."

Michael proved that he was a winner in the next game. The Bulls were losing by one point, with three seconds in the game, when the ball was passed to Michael. There were two Cavaliers trying to intercept the ball, but he grabbed it and skittered away.

And then, with one second left to play, he went airborne.

It's a shot that appears often in highlight films: Michael rising, Craig Ehlo of the Cavs rising, Ehlo descending, and Michael—still aloft—shooting just as the buzzer sounded. The shot was good! The Bulls had won!

The Bulls went on to take the series, and then to defeat

the New York Knicks. For the first time in Michael's pro career, his team was in the conference finals—playing the dreaded Pistons. Michael scored thirty-two points in the first game, fought off the flu to score twenty-seven in the second, and accounted for forty-six points in the third; on the strength of his superhuman efforts, the Bulls led the Pistons, 3-1.

But in game four, Michael's scoring vanished, and in game five, he took only eight shots. It wasn't only that the Jordan Rules were back and working beautifully for Detroit. Coach Collins had criticized Michael for taking more than 30 percent of the team's shots in the play-offs—too many shots, he thought. He wanted Michael to pass more. So Michael did as he was told.

Was that team play? Or was Michael so sensitive that he took even mild criticism as an attack? Which did he want: for the Bulls to win, or for him to be right?

Michael had always said he seemed older than he really was, but this episode raised a question about his maturity. Not in Chicago, however—there he ruled. And so, after the Bulls' now inevitable loss to Detroit, it was clear that something would have to be done to appease the franchise's biggest attraction.

Once again, Michael was the scoring champion. Once again, he was first-team all-NBA. And, once again, he was going to start playing golf a month before he would have liked. But for Michael, the need for a change was even greater than in previous years. For the comparison was louder now: Michael Jordan was like Ernie Banks, the great player for the Chicago Cubs whose team never won a championship and who, because of that, isn't widely remembered as one of the giants of baseball.

CHAPTER EIGHT

WHAT MICHAEL WANTED, Michael got. Although there is no direct evidence that he asked Bulls owner Jerry Reinsdorf to replace his coach, Reinsdorf did just that in the summer of 1989. His replacement for Doug Collins: Phil Jackson, a player on the golden New York Knicks team of the late 1960s and a maverick whose pregame talks tended to mix basketball savvy and lyrics from his favorite musical group, the Grateful Dead.

Maybe it was the possibility of happier times ahead for the Bulls. Or maybe it was the private pleasure he was already taking in his fiancée and his young son. Whatever the reason, Michael overcame his resistance to marriage—at 3:30 in the morning of September 2, 1989, he married Juanita at the Little Wedding Chapel in Las Vegas.

"Juanita had wanted a church wedding," Michael explains. "I said, 'You get me in a church? I'll never do it.' See, I was really nervous. I was afraid too many hands would go up when the preacher said, 'Is there anyone here who thinks these people shouldn't be married?' It wasn't anything I'd done, I just didn't trust my buddies. So I said, 'Let's get it over with.' "

But why 3:30 in the morning?

"We were going to get married the next day," Michael continues. "It was like our bachelor night—we were out gambling, she was with some of her friends, I was with mine, we'd lost our money, and somehow we ran across each other. I told Juanita, 'I'm getting really nervous about this. I just think there will be too many people. If you want to do it, better do it now.' "

So there they were, in jeans, surrounded only by their four closest friends. Michael produced a lovely diamond ring that would have been far too small to impress, say, Elizabeth Taylor. And then, without fanfare, Mr. and Mrs. Jordan flew to California, where Michael was to play in a golf tournament that would benefit the United Negro College Fund.

The ceremony and its aftermath may not sound romantic, but the sheer fact of the marriage was highly significant. For one thing, it reduced his dependence on his mother. This happened in a way that was flattering to Deloris Jordan—Michael compares Juanita to her.

"I trust my wife because she's so much like my

mother," he says. "My mother is businesslike and retiring. Juanita's the same way. Financially, nothing goes past her. She handles the day-to-day financial stuff, and she's got to understand where every dollar goes—if someone comes in with a bill that's not justifiable, he's in for a long day. Because I'm only there as a mediator, and to make the final decision."

On one matter, though, there seems to have been no final decision, just an endless series of postponements. "Before we got married, I told Juanita, 'Who knows? Five years from now, maybe we can do a church wedding,' " Michael says with a chuckle. "And that's what she's banking on— getting married again. She says she was robbed of those precious moments."

Michael and Juanita knew they wanted a large family and a close one. And they knew that "quality time"—spending a few minutes with your loved ones at the end of a busy day—isn't the same thing as a relationship. To nurture a child or really understand a wife requires time and energy and attention. There are no shortcuts. And so, before their marriage, Michael and Juanita reviewed his insanely busy schedule, looking to find ways he could be effective in the world while spending more time at home.

Deloris had suggested one answer: to start the Michael Jordan Foundation as a way to process all the requests for help that came Michael's way. Michael had made much more money than he and his family would ever need; he knew he had an obligation to share his wealth. But a foundation wouldn't just direct his contributions—if it sponsored fund-raisers and enlisted the help of other celebrities, Michael could raise even more money for deserving causes.

Ever since he'd burst into the NBA spotlight, a long line of people had approached him with their hands out. Some represented schools and inner-city charities; others were sick or disadvantaged children who believed their lives would be brightened by a visit, an autograph, or a phone call. Michael read as many of these requests as he could and, without publicity, responded to some of them.

Invariably, he concentrated on requests that involved children. For Michael, kids weren't just his best customers, they were his favorite fans. It was no accident that his first video, *Michael Jordan's Playground*, is built around a kid who dreams of making shots like his idol—and just then, Michael shows up and says, "I know you like playing alone. But do you mind if I shoot with you?" And there were many nights when he would pull off the freeway on his way home from games and, without fanfare, spend an hour hanging out under a streetlight with teenage boys who lived in the troubled housing projects nearby.

Of all the children Michael liked, there was a special

place in his heart for those who were suffering—since the early years of his career, his favorite cause has been the Starlight Foundation, which invites children who are extremely ill to make a wish. For some kids, that wish is going to Disney World, or seeing the ocean, or visiting a relative. For others, it's about meeting an idol—and that idol is, for many of them, Michael Jordan.

"These kids fly into Chicago, they get balls and shirts, they come to a game, and we meet," Michael recalls. "They've been dealing with so much negative stuff, it pleases me to help them see good things. Afterward, I like to keep abreast of them. If I can keep in touch, I do. And I want to know when they pass on, so I can send a note saying how much I enjoyed meeting them."

Listening to Michael talk about these encounters, it's clear that he feels he gets more from the meeting than the kids do. "I like knowing that I can make at least one day special—I can make them smile," he says. "It's humbling for me. Yes, it's sometimes sad. But if I think about it, these kids remind me how fortunate I am."

Having his own foundation made it easier for Michael to deal directly with those unlucky children. His mother kept an eye on a staff that handled requests from institutions and raised money from corporations, so Michael was able to concentrate more on the children's pleas. At the same time, his days weren't quite as busy, so he could be more available to his own family. The Michael Jordan

Foundation looked like a win-win situation—the exact opposite of basketball.

Betty Greer, principal of the Edward T. Hartigan Elementary School, knew exactly what she wanted to do with the $10,000 grant she received from the Jordan Foundation. "Kids can't learn anything or get good grades if they don't come to school," she says. "And in inner-city Chicago, it's really important that we get them here—we don't want them to be tempted by the environment. So I created academic and attendance incentives by starting an awards ceremony."

Each year, thanks to her grant, Greer gives away two bikes for perfect attendance and one hundred trophies for academic excellence. And how does she keep her students focused on these goals? Each week, the homeroom with the best attendance gets to display the basketball that Michael autographed.

Michael's involvement with the Hartigan School goes beyond signing checks and autographing balls. When he learned that one of its students, eleven-year-old Jermone Hale, was suffering from leukemia and dreamed of meeting him, he went right into action. "In the hospital, I could hear but I couldn't see," Jermone recalls. "They leaned over me and said, 'Jermone, guess who's here?' I knew, and I started laughing."

"I know you're real sick, so I won't stay long," Michael

told the boy. "But when you're feeling better, I'd like you to come to a game." And he set a Nike T-shirt, a pair of Air Jordans, and an autographed ball on the bed.

A few months later, Jermone's mother said that this was the night they'd see the Bulls play. They left early for the game. Jermone thought that was so they could get good seats and, perhaps, say hi to Michael. He had no idea what was in store for him. As soon as he settled himself in a seat in the center of the front row, Michael came onto the court and walked right over. "My man, Jermone!" he said. He introduced the boy to Juanita. Then he looked down at the Lakers hat on Jermone's head. "You don't want that around here," he said.

Michael gave Jermone a Bulls hat, then pointed him toward the basket and tossed him a ball. "Put it in the hoop, partner," he said. But Jermone was small and not strong, and every shot was a brick. "You're not leaving until you make a basket," Michael said, and with that, he lifted Jermone over his head so he could dunk.

For many people, gestures like that are a testimony to Michael's ability to remain normal despite his huge celebrity. But in 1989, not everyone was brought to tears by the sight of Michael with a sick child. Some thought these scenes were pure media manipulation—and with good cause. For the first time, Michael was in need of favorable publicity.

In the late 1980s, Michael Jordan shoes and clothes were so highly prized that many kids craved them—and a lot of them couldn't afford them. But that didn't mean they went without Air Jordans and Jordan jackets. According to some school officials, students were stealing their parents' welfare checks in order to buy Jordan products. Even worse were the incidents involving kids who stole Jordan shoes and clothes from other kids; in a ten-week period in Denver, there were forty-five cases of teenagers being robbed of insignia jackets at gunpoint or knifepoint. And on some occasions, weapons were not just displayed—kids were actually willing to kill for Air Jordans.

This violence made critics take a hard look at the Nike commercials directed by Spike Lee. In those ads, Lee played a bicycle messenger from Brooklyn who talked in slang that reflected his inner-city character. White kids and adult sports fans might look at these commercials and think they were cool. For African-American teenagers from the inner city, they were something more—this was practically the first time that they saw kids who looked and talked like themselves on TV. And, according to some columnists, that made Air Jordans irresistible to the very teenagers who were least able to afford them.

The critics also noted the high price of Air Jordans. These shoes were made in Asia, where salaries are very, very low. But Nike was selling them for one hundred dollars. Sure, Jordans were better made than most sneakers that sold for seventy dollars. But were they really thirty dollars better? How, the critics asked, did Nike justify selling its product for such a premium price? Did Nike's responsibility to its customers end at the factory, or did it have an obligation to inject some of the profit from Air Jordans into depressed black communities? What about the social consequences of the inflated price of Air Jordans? Because drugs were the easiest, quickest way for kids in many black neighborhoods to make money, was Nike—as Jesse Jackson claimed—guilty of encouraging drug dealing in the black community?

And it wasn't just shoes. Michael had always been a fan of McDonald's, whose burgers and fries were his favorite treat. Nobody criticized him for that. But when he started making commercials for the fast-food chain, he suddenly came under scrutiny. "Should Michael be encouraging ghetto children to eat hamburgers and french fries when poor nutrition plagues so many of America's poor?" a columnist asked. The unstated answer, of course, was *no*.

Michael Jordan is a commanding presence. His posture is perfect, his clothes are tasteful, his smile is worth every dollar his sponsors pay for it. He doesn't take drugs and never has, he sips only the occasional beer, he rarely curses. It was his custom, after games, to sit in front of his locker and patiently answer questions until every reporter had more than enough Jordan quotes for his story. And his answers were honest; he looked his questioners right in the eye and spoke in a deep, rolling voice that dripped credibility. In that context, he seems to be that rarest of men—a superstar on and off the court.

Until 1989, most of the media people who interviewed Michael were so awed by him that they acted as if they were privileged just to be in the same room. Considering that idol worship, it was unthinkable for them to challenge Michael with questions that had no easy answers. He wasn't paid to be a political activist or a corporate reformer, they seemed to feel. Leave him alone. Cherish him for the greatness of his playing and the example of good living he provides.

In 1989, though, Michael began to lose his immunity from tough questions. One reason was an election in his home state that pitted North Carolina's very conservative senator, Jesse Helms, against a more liberal African-American candidate. It was impossible to believe that Michael would want to see Helms elected to yet another term. But despite a personal appeal from tennis great Arthur Ashe, Michael refused to get involved in this Senate race. Then there was Jesse Jackson's campaign against Nike. As Jackson reminded Jordan, Nike was an almost all-white company, with many African-Americans as endorsers but few as executives and none on its board of directors. He wanted Michael to join his boycott of the company or, at least, speak out about the gap between the company's customers and its executives. Again, Michael maintained a pristine silence.

In another time, Michael could have taken a neutral position without criticism. But in the late 1980s, many African-Americans felt that people of color had been ignored during the eight years of Ronald Reagan's presidency. During those years, the federal government seemed to be giving tax breaks to rich companies and taking away needed services from poor communities. To save money on school lunches, for example, the government had, for a while, decided that ketchup was a vegetable. And the most widely known ingredient in the Reagan plan for curbing drug use was a slogan: "Just say No!"

Now there was a new administration. But to more than a few African-Americans, neither President George Bush nor Vice President Dan Quayle appeared to be very concerned about the problems of the inner city. They, too, seemed to prefer slogans to action. And in 1989, when the vice president spoke before the United Negro College Fund, he didn't even have a firm grip on the group's slogan, "A mind is a terrible thing to waste." Stumbling, Quayle noted, "What a waste it is to lose one's mind, or not to have a mind . . . how true that is."

Episodes like that only increased already chafed sensitivities and put pressure on black celebrities to speak up. Two Michaels—Jordan and Jackson—were then the most celebrated black men in the world. Michael Jackson had created a retreat he called Neverland and, like Peter Pan, seemed to commit himself to eternal boyhood. Michael Jordan, on the other hand, seemed comfortable being a role model.

So it was only natural that the media and African-American leaders would press Michael to step up and talk about issues that were bigger and more complex than basketball. When he wouldn't, it was inevitable that reporters and black leaders alike would begin to ask pointed, fundamental questions about Michael and his motives. Where, they wondered, was Michael's ultimate loyalty—to his people or to the white-owned corporations that had made him rich? At the end of the day, which side was he on?

To Spike Lee, it was outrageous that anyone would criticize Michael Jordan. "Sneakers and jackets and gold chains aren't the cause of violence," he says, his voice tinged with scorn. "That's like saying we should outlaw cars because kids in Newark steal them and start police chases. People ought to get off Michael's back. When he helps the race, he doesn't do it for publicity."

Remembering that season of criticism, Michael sounds just as outraged. Of course he condemned the violence. He even volunteered—a few years after it slowed—to replace any Jordan shoes or clothes that had been stolen. But he insists that this violence had nothing to do with the costly merchandise bearing his name.

"For me, this phenomenon symbolizes the need to reestablish our values in the community from a family standpoint," he says. "We start valuing *things* over life—that's terrible, but it didn't begin with that particular object. It starts at home. When I get criticized because kids get killed for my jackets or shoes, I think that's unfair. But they had to put the blame somewhere instead of looking at themselves, and we were there to take the blame."

It is hardly surprising, therefore, that Michael became cynical about causes and public figures and, most of all, politicians. "I don't sit every day and read everything and learn everything about the people in politics," he told me early in 1993. "I don't think politics is a trustworthy thing. If I had to vote for president, I'd vote for my father. I know, inside and out, what kind of person he is. Anyone else, I'm guessing."

I looked up from my notebook, expecting to see a big grin that would tell me he was kidding. But Michael returned my stare. He wasn't joking. On the contrary. He was proud and angry, and if he was reconsidering what he'd just said, it was only because he was deciding whether he wanted to go on and share any number of other bitter thoughts that he'd been keeping to himself for a long, long time.

CHAPTER NINE

IN THE MIDST of all that conflict, there was also basketball. And that, too, was frustrating for Michael. The 1989–90 Bulls were a superior team, the best that he had played with; Scottie Pippen and Horace Grant had become consistent offensive threats. And Michael was, once again, the league's scoring champion, producing 2,753 points. With all that talent working together, Chicago played exceptionally well–the Bulls' fifty-five wins in the regular season were the second-highest in the history of the franchise.

To those who would be champions, however, the playoffs are the only part of the season that matters. Philadelphia fell to the Bulls in five games, but Chicago's next opponent was Detroit, an opponent that had consistently outplayed them. Detroit easily dominated the Bulls in the first game; at halftime in the second game, with the Bulls trailing 53-38, Michael threw a temper tantrum in the locker room. That wasn't enough to turn things around in the second half, but it did seem to energize the Bulls. They won game three, with Michael contributing forty-seven points, and game four, with Michael pouring in forty-two more. Then Detroit shut Michael down in game five, and the Bulls were on the verge of elimination.

The Bulls roared back to win game six. Now the series was tied, with everything riding on the last game. The pressure was enormous—particularly inside Scottie Pippen's head, where a migraine headache was blurring his vision. Michael had to carry the team, but his thirty-one points weren't enough; the Bulls lost by twenty.

Once again, Michael went off to play golf sooner than he would have liked.

It was a different Michael Jordan who walked into training camp in the fall of 1990. His muscles were bigger—he had started lifting weights with a strength coach—and he wore a gold stud in one ear. In his uniform, he no longer resembled the nice guy Americans knew from the commercials; there was a street toughness about him now.

And there was a new defiance to accompany that look.

To promote Nike products, he'd been to Europe over the summer. "We'd taken Michael to Europe once before, right after he signed with us, and there were two hundred or three hundred people in the stores to meet," Phil Knight recalls. "This time, we had him play some games in arenas. He caused riots. He had to literally fight his way out."

Michael had always known that he was popular in Europe, but now he was intrigued by the possibilities that might flow from his fame. After he retired, he and Nike could, perhaps, own a basketball team in Europe. After he retired, he could have a home in Paris, a city where he could still walk around without causing a riot. After he retired—he'd never thought of that phrase before. Now, for the first time, he was starting to consider how it would feel to achieve his goal of a championship and then escape from the NBA.

If Michael had changed, so had Phil Jackson. The Bulls coach had a radical suggestion for Michael when training camp started—maybe it would be better if he didn't win the scoring title that year. In the past, the Bulls had developed plays but no real system. When the game was on the line, everyone knew Michael would take the big shots; the only time his teammates could reasonably expect to handle the ball was when he was double- or triple-teamed. Now Jackson planned to integrate Michael into the team—he wanted Michael Jordan and the Jordanaires to become, simply, the Bulls.

Michael agreed—grudgingly. If the system worked, he said, he'd go along with it. But if it didn't, he wasn't going to see the team go down in flames while he passed the ball to less reliable shooters. He was, after all, Michael Jordan.

And that meant more, this year, than ever before. For in 1990, he became the king of America's celebrity endorsers, passing Arnold Palmer and Jack Nicklaus—white golfers who were much beloved by white chief executive officers of big corporations—in yearly earnings. That kind of power is intoxicating to any star; it can be deadly for a star who must compete on a team.

And Michael was becoming more and more removed from his fellow Bulls. Riding to road games on the team bus, he wore headphones and dark glasses; his most significant communication with his teammates, some felt, occurred when they were playing cards. The only people Michael seemed consistently happy to see were reporters, and even with them, there was a new edge to his postgame commentary. He was more acid in his criticism of the Bulls general manager. And, that season, he would pick up on a phrase he'd heard and refer to his teammates as "my supporting cast."

There were problems galore with other players that season—Pippen resented his modest salary, Cartwright

and Paxson were waiting to hear if the Bulls wanted to re-
new their contracts, and all eyes turned from time to time
to eastern Europe, where Toni Kukoc wasn't sure he
would accept $2 million to play for Chicago. But control-
ling Michael was going to be Phil Jackson's biggest challenge.

As the season wore on, the conflicts on the team seemed
not to matter. Or maybe it was that open conflict was
preferable to the sniping that might have occurred behind
one another's backs. In any event, the Bulls won games—
sixty-one games, to be exact, their best season ever.

No one expected the Bulls to make it very far in the
play-offs; their record against good teams had been dis-
mal. But in the first round of the play-offs, the Bulls beat
the New York Knicks, 126-85, 89-79, and 103-94—decisive
victories, every one of them. Michael, Horace Grant, and
Scottie Pippen were playing in synch. Bulls fans began to
get excited.

Their next opponent, however, was the Philadelphia
76ers, and that team featured the formidable Charles
Barkley, Michael's good friend and occasional golf partner. These were hard-fought games, and every Bull had to
contribute to keep Chicago's hopes alive. In the final
game, it finally came down to Jordan, who scored thirty-
eight points and made some blistering defensive plays.

And suddenly the Bulls were facing their old nemesis—Detroit.

But this wasn't the same Pistons team that had dominated Chicago in years past. Isiah Thomas had an injured thumb, and the other Detroit starters were also subpar. And no one could have anticipated the coaching trick that Phil Jackson pulled at the start of the fourth quarter of the first game—instead of Michael and the Jordanaires, the Bulls lineup was Horace Grant, B. J. Armstrong, Will Perdue, Cliff Levingston, and Craig Hodges. And that second squad stayed on the court for more than five minutes, turning a three-point lead into a nine-point advantage. When Michael and the first team returned, they would rather have died than squander that lead. Chicago won.

Chicago won the second game. And the third. And, to their delight, the fourth. They had, incredibly, not only beaten Detroit, they had routed the Pistons.

Now, for the NBA championship, the Bulls were to play the Los Angeles Lakers. Michael Jordan vs. Magic Johnson—the two would finally face each other in a showdown more meaningful than an all-star game. The game's reigning superstars. The passer against the slasher. America could hardly wait.

And not just America. This series was to be broadcast in seventy countries. For some players, that pressure would be crushing. But Michael was thinking only about shots that would be heard—and seen, and talked about—around the world.

The series began in Chicago, with what some Bulls regarded as a bad omen: Michael came out firing. He was making his shots, but his teammates weren't getting much of a chance. That wasn't how the Bulls had gotten here. If they reverted to old patterns, Michael would be the game's high scorer—and the Bulls would probably lose.

That did indeed happen. Michael scored thirty-six points, but the effort was so draining that he asked to be taken out for a few minutes during the third quarter. And at the end of the game, with the Bulls down by a point, Michael missed a jump shot that might have sealed a Chicago win. So the Lakers squeaked by.

On the bench, Phil Jackson saw something his players didn't—this Los Angeles team was less than solid. When Magic Johnson wasn't on the court, the Lakers were profoundly second-rate. And Magic was tired from a more grueling play-off ladder than Michael had faced. If he stayed tired, the outcome of the series was all but assured.

In the second game, Chicago played as a team. It showed; after three quarters, they had a massive nineteen-point lead. In the last quarter, Michael scored a basket that has come to be regarded as one of the sport's greatest shots—rising toward the basket for a right-handed dunk, he spotted a defender on his right, flicked the ball into his left hand, and slammed the ball home left-handed. That was the final insult to the Lakers, as Chicago went on to win, 107-86.

The third game was held in Los Angeles, where the Lakers were said to be invincible. Michael was guarding Magic, and both of them seemed determined to prove that the Lakers ruled at home—Michael's shooting was erratic, while Magic was consistently sharp. In the third quarter, without Phil Jackson's permission, Michael and Scottie Pippen changed defensive assignments. The Lakers had been hoping for just this move, and they went on a scoring surge that put them ahead by thirteen points. But the Lakers were an older and more fatigued team, and in the all-important fourth quarter, the Bulls caught up. And at the buzzer, Michael pumped in his predictable last-second miracle to tie the game. Overtime proved to be too much time for the weary Lakers—Chicago coasted to a 104-96 victory.

The Bulls played game four on cruise control. The ball moved crisply around the court, and when it went up, the shooter wasn't always Michael. Los Angeles scored only eighty-two points—the fewest any team had scored in a championship series in ten years—as Chicago took a 3-1 lead. "A nightmare," Magic said.

It got worse for the Lakers. In game five, they played a spirited first half, carrying a one-point lead into the locker room. At the end of the third period, the game was tied. But with seven minutes to play, Michael started passing. He got the ball to Pippen, who hit a three-pointer. He flicked the ball to Paxson, who scored. He found Cartwright, who passed it on to Paxson for yet another basket. And with a minute to go and the Bulls ahead by just two points, Michael decided not to play the hero. He dribbled one way, he dribbled another—and then he tossed the ball to Paxson, whose shot saw nothing but net. The Lakers were finished.

In the locker room, the Bulls said the Lord's Prayer. Then the celebration began. But one man wasn't part of it—holding the trophy as though it were his baby, the Most Valuable Player of the regular season and of the play-offs sat in front of his locker and wept. As his wife and father rubbed his back, the tears continued to flow. At last he began to calm down. But when a friend led Deloris Jordan into the locker room, he started crying again.

"I'm one of the most unemotional people you will ever see—I rarely show emotion," Michael explained later. "But this had been such a struggle. I wanted to be remembered as a champion. But it took eight years. And along the way, there had been so much criticism: 'You can't win with the scoring champion' and 'You can't win without a dominant center.' When I sat in that locker room, all that started playing back in my mind. That was a sweet victory."

It was the last sweet victory he'd experience.

CHAPTER TEN

IN APRIL OF 1991, a month before the play-offs began, Howard White spent an afternoon at Michael's home in the suburbs of Chicago. They were washing the cars, White recalls, when the conversation turned to the subject of Michael's retirement. "If I could win a championship," Michael said, "I could quit."

But a championship is like a potato chip or a piece of candy—it's hard to stop after one. Michael's audience was now vast; his opportunities were limitless. To quit at twenty-eight, just as he was peaking as an athlete and as an endorsement icon, was unthinkable. And so Michael returned to the Bulls, seeking another championship and more corporate sponsors.

His troubles started even before the first game.

*   *   *

It's an American ritual that championship teams visit the White House. The president utters a few banalities. Photographs are taken. And then people go on their way.

But the men and women who create the president's schedule didn't feel that George Bush needed to make a full-court press to meet the Bulls in June of 1991. They decided that a photo of the president surrounded by highly successful African-Americans would be more useful in October, when Bush would be cranking up his reelection campaign. That may have made sense in Washington—but it grated on the biggest attraction in sports.

"I didn't think that date was appropriate, and I thought the team should let them know it wasn't appropriate," Michael told me. "This was *my* time, and now you tell me I've got to go to the White House? That's not right, I'm not going. They knew that—my wife and I wrote them well in advance—but they made it like I stood him up. It wasn't that. First of all, I don't see the reason for sports teams to go to the White House. And I'd met Bush when I was coming out of high school as a McDonald's All-American and he was vice president. I don't think he changed from vice president to president. I mean, he still looked the same. I knew they'd make a political issue out of it, but so what? I'm not obligated to go. I'm not a Republican."

Michael didn't share his political views with the press.

He simply announced that he was having a "family outing" on the day the Bulls grinned down on George Bush. "It's time for me to live my life for myself," he snapped. "I'm tired of living for the media and everybody else."

The image of Michael spending time with Juanita and his two boys—his second son, Marcus James, had been born on Christmas morning of 1990—didn't blunt the criticism of Michael that followed his no-show at the White House. A few of his teammates publicly questioned his decision. A writer for the *Chicago Sun-Times* noted that his snub of the president was "the most disturbing, irresponsible, irrational thing Jordan has ever done in public life."

Michael's real activity on the day his teammates met the president wasn't revealed until mid-December. Michael's family had been nowhere in sight—Michael had been on a golf course in Hilton Head, South Carolina, playing in a foursome that included James "Slim" Bouler, the owner of a golf shop who had once been convicted for dealing cocaine. How did that golf game become public? Because when federal officials had arrested Bouler, he had been in possession of piles of money. How did Bouler come to have all that cash? According to Bouler, $57,000 of it was a "loan" from Michael Jordan.

When asked, Michael confirmed Bouler's story. That was foolish. As Michael well knew, that $57,000 was no loan. And, because he lied about it, that $57,000 became a ticking bomb, poised to blow up his unblemished reputation.

Michael had a second embarrassing problem that fall. Sam Smith, a reporter for the *Chicago Tribune*, had followed the Bulls during their run for the championship. He had hung out in the locker room and privately interviewed a number of Michael's teammates. Now he was publishing a diary of the 1990–91 season called *The Jordan Rules*, and if advance excerpts were any indication of the book's tone, Michael wouldn't take much pleasure from reading it.

For the Michael Jordan of *The Jordan Rules* wasn't the Michael Jordan the public knew—a happy-go-lucky guy who only turned fierce when he stepped onto the court. In these pages, Michael was a moody, pampered superstar who dominated his teammates so completely that he once punched Will Perdue in practice. Now his teammates— and some Bulls executives—were taking a very public revenge on their superstar.

"I have a dream: I'm going to get the ball," Horace Grant told Smith. B. J. Armstrong put it another way: "I'd never played before without the ball." According to Smith, cocaptain Bill Cartwright wouldn't go along with Michael's edict that no one should pass to the low-scoring center in the final minutes: "If I ever hear again that you're telling guys not to pass me the ball," Cartwright told Michael, "you will never play basketball again." The general manager was said to have moaned that if the Bulls had only managed to draft Hakeem Olajuwon, they would have won two NBA championships by 1989. Pretty much everybody, it seemed, believed that Michael played for himself, not for the good of the team.

Michael was horrified. "Some of that book was true—but there was no explanation from my standpoint," he says. " 'Why were you yelling at Horace? Why didn't Bill Cartwright get the ball?' If Smith had asked about any of those points, I would have answered—remember, I didn't know what the book was about. If I thought it was about my impact on the team, I would have given him my insights, but Smith never talked to me about that."

Michael felt surrounded by hostile forces. Were his teammates really enemies with smiling faces? How could he defend himself from their accusations without getting caught up in more lies? As *The Jordan Rules* rolled into bookstores, what new revelations might emerge to damage him?

Help came from an unexpected source. Shortly before Christmas in 1991, the Lakers arrived in Chicago for a game that many fans thought would be a heated rematch. But the game was overshadowed by a press conference called by those two archrivals Michael Jordan and Magic Johnson.

Because Magic had recently announced that he was HIV-positive, some expected an announcement about a joint effort to raise money for AIDS research. Instead, Magic made a direct and eloquent plea to the media— Michael is a national treasure, don't run him out of basketball.

But the news business takes no prisoners. Scandal sells newspapers and magazines. Already, Michael had been knocked off his pedestal. A few more headlines, and he might be knocked right out of the game.

"I have a right to associate with whomever I choose," Michael said. His lawyer, David Falk, disagreed. "Michael is human, and he will make mistakes, and I felt he needed to acknowledge that," he explained in 1993. "Others—I won't mention names, but one is a national leader—said he didn't need to apologize. I told Michael, 'If you want to be a role model, I don't think you have the right to associate with anyone you want. This isn't a heinous crime. It's an error in judgment. It won't kill you to admit it.' "

So Michael held a press conference and apologized. He acknowledged that the $57,000 represented gambling losses on golf. And he said that a celebrity who's willing to be cast as a role model has a special obligation to be squeaky-clean.

"That was a maturing experience," Jordan told me. "I don't want to play golf with drug dealers. I don't want to be around drug dealers because I don't think they're a positive influence. But you don't know who's a drug dealer today—they don't all wear gold chains. How do I pick my golf partners now? No third parties. I have people who run checks on people. I have to check who's coming into my house and who I talk to. I feel like *I'm* the damn president. That's the part of this life I don't really like."

Michael may have been wrong to associate with dubious characters, but when NBA officials suggested they might investigate his gambling, he was furious. Didn't the league understand? He was a prisoner—of his ability, his fame, and of society's impossible demands. If he placed a friendly bet on a round of golf or a game of cards, who got hurt? Wasn't he entitled to have a private life? What would the NBA prefer—that he cheated on his wife, or drank, or took drugs?

Increasingly, Michael found all scrutiny intolerable. As he looked for a way out, one solution had great appeal— to become less accessible. In postgame interviews, he still gave reporters what they needed. He never missed a photo shoot or the filming of a commercial. But in his private life, he slammed the curtain down. One of the most familiar faces on the planet belonged to a virtual hermit.

"A few years ago, I lost the desire to go out," Michael admitted in 1993. "Shopping malls are out of the question. I think I go to a mall only for Christmas; I don't want a personal shopper and all that. Mostly, I'm at home, listening to music and watching TV all day. Or I spend the afternoon sleeping on the couch at my mother-in-law's house and eating her old-fashioned macaroni and cheese. Then comes the game. And my wife doesn't want to go right home after the game. So I have to call ahead to restaurants: 'Are you closing? Can we get a private room where no one will bother us, not even the waitress?' I think my wife deserves that attention from me. So we do that . . . maybe twice a month. And that's a lot."

His isolation had a predictable side effect: Michael no longer cared what people he could never hope to please had to say about him. That was why, alone among NBA players, Michael chose to do the unthinkable—with Nike, he sued the NBA.

The way the Jordan camp saw it, so many Americans had become interested in basketball because of Michael that the league had been able to add several new teams, and those teams brought in more revenue to the NBA. Thanks to Michael, the value of the NBA's television contracts had soared. Thanks to Michael, T-shirts and other items authorized by the NBA had produced millions more in revenues.

Michael got none of that money. No player did. Some of it, according to the NBA, went into a players' retirement fund. For most players, that arrangement was fine;

they had done little to generate this additional income.

But Michael's situation was different. Each year, thanks again to him, NBA-endorsed firms sold about $400 million worth of products bearing the image or uniform number of Michael Jordan or the team logo of the Bulls. Michael would have had to be superhuman not to care about royalties from a business of that magnitude.

It wasn't just money that bothered Michael. To him, the NBA was irresponsible. To keep his image from becoming so widely seen that people tired of him, Michael had turned down lucrative offers for his face to appear on lunch boxes. He had said no thanks to a company that wanted to produce Michael Jordan soap-on-a-rope.

But the NBA seemed willing to accept even the most inappropriate offer—as long as the money rolled in. The Michael Jordan beer-can cooler was an example. Michael cared too much about his young fans to appear in a beer commercial. And yet the NBA allowed a company to make and sell a beer-can cooler in the shape of his head: Open Michael's scalp, and out pops a cool can.

For Phil Knight and Nike, deciding to fight the NBA took little soul-searching. "It was a simple issue for us," Knight says. "The NBA had effectively stolen—for lack of a better word—rights that Michael had assigned to us. And each year, they were getting more aggressive in their marketing of those stolen rights."

Michael knew he would look greedy if he fought the

league. But the ultimate issue was his integrity: "I'd given Nike my word that they'd have exclusive rights to my line. And yet my name was being used—and overused—by the NBA. They were selling T-shirts that were affecting sales of my Nike T-shirts. I felt someone had to take a stand."

The result was a long, hard fight with the NBA, which ended with the league agreeing to return Michael's rights to him. To protect its interests in the future, Nike went into the business of managing players. Nike promptly became so powerful in this new arena that when Alonzo Mourning was asked whom he played for, the Charlotte Hornets or Nike, he replied, "Nike."

One final result—at the 1992 all-star game, the NBA T-shirts featured every player except Michael. And as Michael had anticipated, "I did get labeled a greedy guy."

As long as Michael was in a fighting mood, he told the NBA that he saw no reason why he should play on the American basketball team in the 1992 Olympics. He'd had that thrill in 1984, he said; it was time for college stars and young professionals to represent their country in Barcelona. But the Olympic committee wouldn't be put off. This was to be a "Dream Team," guided by former Detroit Pistons coach Chuck Daly and starring Larry Bird, Carl Malone, Charles Barkley, Patrick Ewing, David

Robinson, John Stockton—even Magic Johnson. Such a team wouldn't be complete without Michael.

That roster made the difference. "I wanted to see what kind of people the other guys were: if their practice habits were the same as mine, if they worked as hard as I did," Michael says. Additionally, he was lured by a once-in-a-lifetime chance to play alongside Magic. And, some say, he couldn't resist an opportunity to make the ultimate all-star team—and use his influence to keep Isiah Thomas, who expected Chuck Daly to add him to the team, thousands of miles from Barcelona.

But there was a significant roadblock in the way: business. Michael endorsed Wheaties, and Olympic teams are featured on boxes of Kellogg's cereal. And at the Olympics, the most celebrated name associated with Nike would be expected to wear uniforms and warm-up suits with Reebok insignia.

Michael didn't want to betray companies he endorsed, so he consulted with Wheaties and Nike. "Wheaties wasn't going to let me do Kellogg's," he recalls. "Nike said, 'Because there are so many other guys—David Robinson and John Stockton—in the same situation, it's not that big a deal.'" Michael took those reactions back to the Olympic committee. And that committee, he says, couldn't have been more reassuring: "They told me, 'Oh, don't worry about it. Just sign this release form. We'll have a compromise by the time you have to stand up and get your medal.' "

On the strength of that promise, he says, he joined the Dream Team.

Now, Michael believed, only one problem was ahead—winning a second straight championship. And, along the way, being named Most Valuable Player in the regular season and in the play-offs. No one had ever accomplished those three goals; he wanted to be the first.

But Michael's motivation wasn't the thrill of a unique achievement. It was revenge. "I want a championship worse this year than last, because I want to prove to people that those jerks can't hold me down," Michael told writer Bob Greene, not bothering to name all those in the press and the NBA who had annoyed him in the past few years. "It would prove that it's they who are lacking, not me. Nothing I could say out loud would answer how I feel about them more than winning a second championship would."

Chicago came out of the gate fast that season, with a fourteen-game winning streak. When *The Jordan Rules* was officially published, Michael went into a month-long slump. But the Bulls kept on rolling, adding a thirteen-game winning streak to their amazingly strong record.

In March, though, there was another nonbasketball story about Michael. A North Carolina bail bondsman was murdered, and in his wallet, police found photocopies of checks written by Michael Jordan that totaled $108,000. It turned out that the murder victim was one of the players in that South Carolina golf game. This was no longer innocent gambling between friends—the NBA not only investigated this incident, but reprimanded Michael. This time, Michael made his anger work for him; he played brilliantly at the end of the regular season, leading the Bulls to a best-ever 67-15 record.

Chicago swept a young and inexperienced Miami team in the first round of the play-offs, then moved on to New York. Pat Riley had molded the Knicks into a well-conditioned team that wasn't afraid to play an intensely physical game and talk trash to opponents. Xavier McDaniel, for one, went right at Scottie Pippen, intimidating him with pushes and shoves that had Pippen cringing. The Knicks won that first game, the Bulls the second. Michael provided the memorable moment in the Bulls' victory in game three when he thrust a fist at McDaniel and Patrick Ewing after slicing between them for a layup. But the Knicks won game four to tie the series at 2-2. The teams split the next two games—this rivalry was going to require the full string.

Michael came out in game seven ready to fire his team up. His method: to intimidate McDaniel at the earliest opportunity. "A lot of the other guys were tentative, so I felt I had to stand up—even though this guy could give me a black eye or kick my ass, I had to make that statement," he explains. "We were basically cursing each other out. Then I looked at the referee and said, 'I hope there won't be a fight, because I don't think I can win.' And the referee laughed. It was like standing up to a bully—McDaniel didn't really want a fight. And from that point on, there really wasn't a problem. I felt that was a crucial play from Horace and Scottie's standpoint. They could have been intimidated by physical players, but that time they stood up."

So did the other Bulls, as Chicago romped to an easy 110-81 victory and the right to face Cleveland in the conference finals. It took six games—and Michael had to score sixteen points in the final quarter of game six to do it—but the Bulls once again prevailed. Now it was time to face the Portland Trail Blazers for the championship.

Once again, Michael was best when the challenge was greatest. In the first game, Michael was in a zone, shooting three-pointers as if they were foul shots. He made basketball look easy as he bombed one long shot after another. By the end of the second quarter, he'd scored a half-game finals record of thirty-five points, including six three-pointers—and even Michael had to shake his head in wonder. The Bulls won, 122-89. And went on to take their second straight championship five games later.

This time, the NBA's Most Valuable Player and Most Valuable Player of the championship series didn't weep. He stood on the scorer's table, dancing to the music and pumping his fist at the happy crowd in Chicago Stadium. And then it was on to the locker room, where he was once again doused with champagne. He didn't care. As he flopped onto a bench, brandishing a huge unlit cigar, he and Scottie Pippen howled like dogs.

This, he seemed to be saying, is how it works out when everybody leaves me alone.

CHAPTER ELEVEN

IN BARCELONA, Michael returned to earth with a thud. The Olympic committee hadn't told him the truth. There wasn't any compromise. There was just a Code of Conduct card, which was a sentence to the effect that he would wear his country's dress uniform—with the Reebok insignia—whenever the coach ordered. Michael understood exactly what it meant: Either wear the Reeboks or you don't pick up your gold medal.

Before he formally refused to go along with the program, he checked in with Nike. "My loyalty is to you," he told Phil Knight. "So I'm going to stick with my decision. I've never stuck with an issue publicly—or made an issue. I've always straddled the fence. But this time, I'm going to make a stand."

Knight appreciated Michael's commitment. But he was

worried for Michael. "You're going to get criticized quite a bit," he said. "It's not worth it."

Michael was philosophical. "This is one time I'm going to see what happens," he replied.

He wasn't alone. "I have two million reasons not to wear Reebok," cracked Charles Barkley, referring to the $2 million that he received each year from Nike.

Barkley, who's known for speaking his mind, certainly blurted out the truth that time—in Barcelona, money ultimately talked louder than patriotism. Because Team Nike wouldn't budge, Team USA had to give in. The Nike athletes would wear the official uniforms when they accepted their medals, but they could drape American flags over the Reebok logos they found so offensive.

Now all they had to do was win.

Michael was certainly relaxed enough during the practice sessions in Monte Carlo. During the day, he and Charles played golf. In the evening, they turned dinners into laughfests. "The closest I've ever been to royalty before was Michael Jordan," Barkley remarked when he met Prince Rainier of Monaco. Later, they haunted the casinos and talked trash to the blackjack dealers. "I hated the way they deal, so I told them, 'This is robbery, we can't win,' " Michael says. "But there was nothing else to do at night, so we kept on playing—and got killed."

Practice was a different story. These were men who knew far more than they ever wanted to learn about the business of sports. Now, in the security of a gym, they could finally put all that down and enjoy the game they once played for free. Basketball was pure here, and, once again, they were boys, fooling around without any thoughts of reputations or business. Underneath the insults, behind the banter, there was love—this was an elite fraternity that had never before been able to meet like this. They played H-O-R-S-E. They compared trick shots. And then they settled in for some serious intersquad scrimmages.

"The competitive attitude was so high, it was the ultimate pickup game," Michael recalled in 1993, still savoring his memories of the previous summer. "Some guys got the emotion from standing on the podium, but for me, the joy was in the practice. Everything else was a down. I just loved it."

He especially prized the time with Magic Johnson, the self-appointed "big dog" of the team. "Earvin and I have had a difficult friendship," he told me. "The way I came into the league, I had a lot of notoriety and success before I'd proven anything. And off the court, I jumped into the league and got ahead of him. He had envy, jealousy, all that—he thought he should be getting what I was getting. But I didn't control that, and I think that's something he found out. So the Olympics was my way of getting to know him better, because he was retired now and there's no telling where his life is going to lead him."

With all that emotion flowing, the games themselves were anticlimactic—the Dream Team dazzled their opponents and won every contest, usually by a huge margin. And when it was over, the awards ceremony provoked no controversy. But for Michael, all the victories in Barcelona seemed less important than the good fellowship, the chance to play without pressure or scrutiny, and the sheer pleasure of walking the streets without worrying that the crowd following him would turn into a mob.

"My wife and I have to have a life of our own, and we have to be relaxed while we're doing it," he said in Barcelona. "Here, if I want to go into a bar and have a beer, I do it. I've learned that being perfect is something you *can't* do. I'm glad the bubble burst."

As the 1992–93 season started, Michael could hardly believe it. "After playing all the way into June, then all summer with the Olympic team, I didn't want to see the ball," he told me. "It's like, 'Hey, I'm *already* back here?' " Boredom and fatigue, though, were his only worries: "Because we'd done something twice, I thought the pressure would be off the third time. I thought the season would be easy."

It was anything but. At midseason, the Bulls had the best record in their conference, but they also had dissension and fatigue. B. J. Armstrong went from the starting lineup to the bench, he said, after Michael and Scottie Pippen claimed he was taking too many shots. Horace Grant had a different complaint—not enough shots. "I don't want to finish my career known as a guy who has done all the dirty work," he said. With Michael as the only Bull anyone seemed to notice, Stacy King, Will Perdue, and Scott Williams all asked to be traded.

What they didn't know was that Michael was even more troubled than they were.

"I want to set things up for when I step away from the game," Michael said as we began our first interview session. "Magic and Larry Bird are gone, and those guys were driving forces for me. I was just a notch below them in everybody's expectations. When they left, that put me in the top notch—and who drives me?"

"Maybe all the players who want what you have," I suggested.

He nodded. "That's what I found as a motivator—people trying to catch me. My challenge now is to keep some space between them and me. To win a third championship, that's another challenge. But the driving forces are getting limited."

Michael and Juanita had just had a third child, a daughter named Jasmine. And here was Michael, trapped in a Dallas hotel, connected to his family only by phone. I wondered if the loneliness of his job wasn't getting more acute as his family grew.

"I realize how much my kids change while I'm gone," he said, explaining that he would retire when they were of school age. And when he retired, he said, he would no longer be a public figure. "I don't want to stay out there, or be on television. I have contracts I'll have to maintain, but I want to do it in a low-key way. I feel like a lot of fans: I'm starting to hear Michael Jordan's name maybe too much. For the last four or five years, I've been up there, and every week, on the TV, there's a Michael Jordan ad. I can understand people getting tired of that. Sure, there are days when I'm in the mood to live the part, to be 'Michael Jordan.' But those days are becoming fewer and fewer."

The greatest athletes often have the most difficulty thinking about the end of their career. Michael, however, couldn't stop thinking about retiring. "At some point in time, my career and the shoe business will take a downfall," he said, with no bitterness or regret. "That's one reason, from a business standpoint, why some people try to maximize the situation at hand. Because they're not going to keep on playing that well. You can see the writing: 'hitting his peak now, maybe at the tail end of his career, you never know, he's played a lot of minutes and done a lot of things.' That's not me. I don't think I can mentally accept taking a step back. Come off the bench—I don't think I could ever do that. My whole career, I've been a starter. You ask me to play twenty minutes in certain situations, I can't accept that. When the guys I passed start passing me, I'll leave."

*   *   *

In that spirit of realism, Michael was using our conversations to demolish several of the key myths that have sprung up about him over the years. The "Air Jordan" label, first and foremost. The world likes to believe that Michael can fly—that when he goes up for a shot, his "hang time" lasts so long because he has, for all practical purposes, defied the laws of gravity.

"There is no such thing as 'hang time,' " Michael insisted. "It's an illusion."

"But a Nike commercial," I pointed out, "has a scientist explain what you achieve as 'a low-earth orbit off the vertical plane.' "

"It's an illusion," Michael repeated. "The way I move my body, it looks like I'm hanging. I may jump higher than most people, but I don't hang. It's just an illusion created by the motion of my legs and arms."

Something does happen when Michael goes up for a shot. But because of all the excitement about "hang time," no one ever asks about it. That's unfortunate, for it's just as amazing—and far more useful for fans to know about. It's this: When Michael shoots, time seems to slow down.

"I have great vision and focus," Michael explained, "and as I go up, I can see myself doing a lot of different things with the greatest of ease. And that gives me the kind of patience other people have only in normal situations. A lot of people, in pressure situations, tend to speed up. I remain calm. I don't force the issue—if you have to force it, I don't think it's going to happen."

And now, in the same way that time blurred as Michael approached the basket, our conversation broadened until we weren't talking so much about basketball as about life.

"It's part of the success thing I've gone through my whole life," Michael said. "You wake up as a kid and you chase something, you chase stardom—you're never going to get it. When you least expect it, it happens. That's one of the things I want to teach my kids: I don't want to force them to go after stardom. If they get it, it just happens. I see a lot of kids—kids who ask me for autographs, who come to the camps—who have these dreams of becoming professional players. I know it won't happen. It's bestowed on you when you least expect it, you can't chase it."

I understood what he meant, but I was stuck—as so many are—on the subject of "hang time." I wasn't one of those who believed that Michael had special powers. But I had come to think of Michael as an athlete who had taken his game to a level beyond sports; he had become an artist, right up there with the greats of painting and music and writing. In that realm, I imagined, Michael might not be able to fly—but surely he could float.

"I've looked at a lot of film," Michael said softly, knowing he was puncturing this illusion for good, "and

I've slowed it down, and it's just an act of leg movement, a way of spreading my legs so they look like wings. But I'm still going up and coming down."

"Maybe it's because we've never seen anything like this," I suggested. "So when you're coming down, it still looks to us as if you're going up."

"That's right."

"And looking as if you're still going up when the fact is you're coming down—that's the theme of what we're talking about anyway, isn't it?"

"Exactly," Michael said.

The sense that the world was going one way and Michael was going another surfaced again a month later, when I went with him to the "shoe lab" at Nike headquarters in Beaverton, Oregon. The Nike designers had been working on the 1994 model of Air Jordans, and now they were ready for Michael's comments. The shoes were uncomplicated and unthreatening, very much in the pared-down spirit of the current style. They were easy to like, and Michael quickly approved them.

Then Tinker Hatfield, head of the Jordan design squad, had a surprise.

"Would you like to pull out of Nike and have your own brand?" Hatfield asked, pulling out designs for a complete line of Michael Jordan clothes and shoes.

I looked over at Michael. Wasn't this almost exactly

what Rob Strasser and Peter Moore had wanted to do in 1988?

"We've been talking about this a long time," Michael dryly reminded the Nike design team.

"It's the way I've always wanted to go," Hatfield said. "I'm with you."

There was laughter, and then there was, for the briefest moment, a poignant silence. These people knew Michael and his sometimes tempestuous history with Nike. And they had to sense this offer might not have been made if Michael planned to play deep into the future. For these were leisure clothes, not athletic gear—the very existence of those designs was acknowledgment that he was entering the fourth quarter of his career.

CHAPTER TWELVE

$\mathbf{M}$ICHAEL CERTAINLY didn't play as if his career was winding down. Night after night, he was the toughest Bull of them all, ignoring his own injuries and fatigue to average forty minutes on the court in the regular season and a stunning forty-five minutes in the play-offs. "I have seen Michael almost unable to walk, and yet he'll play the next day," marvels Howard White. "Or his wrist will be so swollen that he can't bend it. He'll say, 'Don't worry about me,' and go out and make the big rebound, the big steal, the big shot. I've never seen anyone so mentally tough."

Michael began to redirect that toughness at the all-star game in February of 1993. As was his custom, he skipped the mandatory press conference to play golf on a private course in Las Vegas. For that, as was its custom, the NBA fined him. "I told them weeks ago I wouldn't make it,"

Michael said airily. "I needed some time to take it easy and enjoy my thirtieth birthday. And what's the fine going to be, a few dollars?"

Then Michael dropped a big hint: "I want to step back from the public eye." He went even further when he was asked about his enthusiastic support of Shaquille O'Neal, the first rookie elected to the all-star starting team since he had won that honor in 1985. "I didn't want Shaq to go through what I did as a rookie," he said. "I want to usher him in as I close in on retirement."

If no one realized that Michael was tipping his plan to retire sooner rather than later, there was good reason. He effortlessly scored thirty points in the all-star game, and, in Chicago's next confrontation with O'Neal's team, he went on a shooting spree that reduced the huge center with the size twenty sneakers to a babbling spectator. "You look at Michael, and he does things, and you say, 'He *didn't* do that,' " O'Neal gushed after that game. "But when he hits for sixty-four points against us, you know this guy's for real. If I were a fan, I'd pay to see Michael Jordan."

For all his weariness, Michael's game grew even tougher and deadlier as the season rolled on. He led Chicago to the best record of any eastern division team during the regular season, as well as to sweeps of Atlanta and Cleveland in the opening rounds of the finals. The last few seconds of the clinching victory over Cleveland were grist for an ever-lengthening highlight film—Michael got the ball with eighteen seconds on the clock and the score tied, dribbled toward the basket, and then turned his back on the net. When there were just three seconds left, he wheeled around and tossed up a fadeaway jumper that dropped through the net as the buzzer sounded. The Cleveland coach resigned a week later.

The Bulls knew that the New York series would be a grudge match, with the Knicks determined to derail Chicago's three-peat express. And, in a curious way, the Bulls knew they were the underdogs in this series. The New York team was in peak condition; Scottie Pippen and Michael, in contrast, had been playing basketball almost nonstop for twenty months. In their regular season games, Pat Riley's team had consistently outplayed the Bulls. To say the Knicks smelled blood was to understate the case.

The Bulls lost the first game in New York, perhaps because Michael was tired and missed seventeen of his twenty-seven shots. Michael has no use for the city of New York—"I hate it, I think it's overcrowded and dangerous; too many people are bunched up, and things can happen," he told me—and so, to relax before game two, he and his father and some friends spent the evening in Atlantic City. There he lost $5,000 at the blackjack tables. But his gambling was less of an issue than the time he went to bed. Although an Atlantic City hotel employee said Michael left around 11 P.M., others said they saw him in the casino at 2:30 A.M.

"I was back in New York and in bed at one o'clock," Michael told reporters after his unusual night out made headlines. "Let me see one person say I was there at one o'clock, and they'd have a lawsuit. I was just trying to get away from New York and relax, instead of sitting there and listening to the media hype about the first game." Michael also commented on what he felt was the unfairness of the press: "If my life comes to the point where I'm scrutinized about what I do in my free time, then there's no need to even talk to you guys."

The reporters had more questions, however: Was this new incident linked to Michael's gambling on golf and cards? Did Michael think he had a gambling problem? "That's it," Michael snapped, and stalked off. He would not, the team spokesman announced, be talking to reporters again during the play-offs.

But criticism of Michael's casino visit didn't die down—that night, the Bulls lost the second game, 96-91. Although Michael scored thirty-six points in that game, another statistic seemed more significant: He missed twenty of his thirty-two field goal attempts, many of them at the end of the game.

If Michael had stayed in his hotel room, some sportswriters suggested, he might not have been so weary in the fourth quarter. They went on to note that no team had come back from a 0-2 deficit in the play-offs and won in sixteen years. Was Michael so supremely confident that he felt he could roll dice against history?

In the storm of personal criticism that followed this loss, Michael's father became his spokesman, and an outraged one at that. "Giving his all last summer playing in the Olympics—which he didn't want to do—and then coming right back has been hard on him, but he's done it without complaining," James Jordan said. "He has sacrificed to try and satisfy everybody, and after doing all of that, people still find a way of knocking him. How much is enough? How much does he have to give?"

Michael chose to provide his answer on the court in game three, as the team that Coach Jackson was calling the "grimmer, darker" Bulls went out to try and win their first game. Michael seemed to be keeping his distance from the basket as well as from the media—he sank only three of his eighteen field goal attempts. But he made his presence felt by passing to his unguarded teammates, who, as it turned out, were expert shots. When it was over, the Bulls had overwhelmed the Knicks by twenty points, 103-83.

Michael was still freezing the media out, but he was blazing on the court in game four. Shooting often from three-point range and going up for closer shots with defenders swarming over him, he went on a scoring spree that's unusual in play-off competition. Seventeen points in the first period. Ten in the second. In the third, he made his first seven shots, ending up with eighteen for the period. If he faltered in the last quarter, it was only because he had five fouls and needed to be taken out of the game for a few minutes. Grand total: fifty-four points, just a basket short of his best performance in a regulation-length play-off game. Naturally, the Bulls won, 105-95, to tie the series.

The Bulls took the fifth game in a squeaker that saw Michael score "only" twenty-nine points, and wrapped the series up in the sixth game, with Michael scoring twenty-four. Now it was on to Phoenix, where the only man between Michael and a third consecutive championship ring was Charles Barkley, his best friend in basketball.

Once again, though, sporting competition took second place to Michael's personal life. Just before game six of the Knicks series, a California businessman named Richard Esquinas released a book that he published himself called *Michael and Me: Our Gambling Addiction . . . My Cry for Help!* In it, he said that he and Michael had not only been frequent golf partners but had bet on their games, sometimes as much as $250,000 on a single shot.

They had, Esquinas claimed, played for money in October of 1991—the same month Michael gambled on golf with a convicted drug dealer—and Michael lost $626,000. According to Esquinas, Michael then doubled the bet and lost. At that point, he said, Michael owed him $1.3 million.

Esquinas said that Michael later won a few games, reducing his debt to $902,000. But Michael didn't want to pay up, he continued, so they negotiated a settlement of $300,000. To date, Michael had paid $200,000.

Michael was livid, both at the timing of the Esquinas book and the allegations. "I have played golf with Richard Esquinas, with wagers made between us," he said in a statement that confirmed the payment of $200,000. "Because I didn't keep records, I cannot verify how much I won or lost. I can assure you the level of our wagers was substantially less than the preposterous amounts that have been reported."

He went on to label Esquinas "a former friend" who had exploited their relationship by publicizing it at a moment when he could sell his book. And so, Michael announced, he saw no reason to pay Esquinas another penny. The harshest judgment, he seemed to suggest, should be reserved for Esquinas, not him.

That reminded me of a conversation Michael and I had about gambling just five months earlier. I had seen a video of him playing a card game called Tonk with his teammates in the waiting room of an airport. "This is a winner, I'm gonna get rich—I'll make thirty million, these are my pigeons!" Michael chortles in that video. "This is fun!"

When I reminded him of that video, Michael smiled. "I was winning," he said.

"Tonk is a game you've taught to other players?" I asked.

"They all know it."

"Someone told me a story about you playing with a rookie, and him losing a lot, and you making him pay," I said.

Michael nodded. "Everybody learns lessons," he replied. "This was a lesson he had to pay for, just as I had to pay when I came in. That's one thing about the league: You pass lessons down. As rookies come in, you teach them the way of the game. That's how it works."

But the lessons he had learned and taught didn't seem to apply for Michael in the matter of his debt to Richard Esquinas. Nor were the Bulls eager to find out the extent of Michael's gambling—Bulls management took the position that, until it was proven that Michael had violated a league rule or committed a crime, his private life was a private matter.

That was a minority view. Everyone else weighed in with opinions on the subject, some suggesting that Michael really was addicted to gambling, others asking if role models were allowed to be human. But there were also commentators who declined to moralize—to them, this controversy was becoming much too serious. "Does Michael Jordan stand for something more than basketball and sneakers?" asked Robert Lipsyte in the *New York Times*. "Did Ted Williams or Arnold Palmer? Isn't it all in our minds, anyway?"

That was one sports column Michael could almost have written himself. "People are trying to make it seem like I have a gambling problem," he said when he broke his silence the following week. "It's a hobby. I enjoy it. If I had a problem, I'd be hocking my watch, my championship rings, I'd sell my house. If I bet a million, that would be sick. But so what if I bet half a million? I'm not broke. I'm happy. I'm at peace with myself, more or less. I know what my motives are now—making history, basketballwise."

"He has no weaknesses," moaned Dan Majerle of the Phoenix Suns. "You can't play Michael to drive, you can't play him for his jump shots, you can't shade him to his left or his right. His first step is so quick, you can't keep him from going by you. You try to deny him the ball, but if you play him too tight, he'll go backdoor on you. You just have to make him work hard and do your best—and most of the time, your best isn't good enough."

Now, against Phoenix, Michael's best was about to get

even better. "Michael couldn't wait to play basketball after Atlantic City," Magic Johnson explained. "He couldn't wait to play basketball after this guy came out with this book. That's where you solve all your problems—on the court."

Michael's scoring against Phoenix is proof of his ability to do just that: thirty-one points in the first game, then forty-two, forty-four, fifty-five, forty-four, and thirty-three. But beyond those record-breaking numbers was the human factor. For this series was like a recap of all the issues that had plagued Michael throughout his career.

Taking every shot possible: At one point, Michael took ten in a row.

Making the big basket: With time running out, Michael won a game with a one-handed floater as he was being fouled by Charles Barkley.

And surprising everyone with unselfish play: The winning basket in the final game wasn't scored by Michael but by John Paxson, who swished a three-pointer to seal the victory.

In the pandemonium that followed, Michael was the Bull with the greatest presence of mind—before he ran off the court, he made sure he grabbed the ball. Having achieved this championship and established these scoring records in the finals, he knew he had truly made history. At the least, he had finally surpassed Magic and blown by Bird. At the most, he'd set a standard so high that no one playing now would erase it. "I'm not campaigning for the best player in the world, or in history," he said that night. "But I think this means a lot."

Michael was too tired, though, to think more about it just then. "I don't want to see another basketball, another referee, or another reporter," he said. "All I want to see are my wife and kids."

CHAPTER THIRTEEN

Michael MAY HAVE BEEN the unquestioned emperor of basketball in 1993, but he had very limited powers. He opened a restaurant bearing his name in Chicago, and his fans lined up around the block. In a hamburger commercial, he joked that he wanted a Big Mac much more than a fourth championship. He played golf with Arnold Palmer in a pro-am tournament and, after nine holes, held a one-stroke lead over one of the masters of the links.

But he couldn't stop the buzz about his gambling.

Charles Barkley made a joke of it. Michael had offered to make him a present of a car, a Ferrari Testarossa. How much, he was asked, does that car cost? "I think $100,000, or maybe $200,000—or just a couple of golf rounds," Barkley quipped before quickly adding, "Just kidding, I was just kidding."

Jerry Reinsdorf had seen it firsthand, and also had a humorous context for it. "Flying back from Portland on the team plane, I saw him playing cards with a stack of bills in front of him," the Bulls owner told me a few months before Michael's gambling made headlines. "Later, I came by and said, 'The stack is going down.' Michael looked up and said, 'Yes, but the bills are bigger.' "

Lawrence Taylor, the legendary linebacker for the New York Giants, was annoyed that he had been dragged into the controversy by Richard Esquinas but amused by the reported size of the bets. Yes, he said, he had played golf for money with Michael. But he had lost "substantially less" than the $150,000 that Esquinas had claimed. "Believe me, I'll gamble on some golf, but money comes a little harder to me than it does to Michael," Taylor said. "The amount we bet wouldn't even make a good poker ante."

Michael's father, seeking to calm the waters, explained that Michael "used his money to buy competition." David Stern, commissioner of the NBA, tried to put the issue in perspective: "I know a lot of people who, when the stock market crashed, lost a lot of money, and we didn't do an audit on them." But in mid-July, the controversy hadn't gone away—and Michael decided he had to go on television to try and put the stories to rest.

"I can stop gambling," he insisted on *Eye to Eye* when Connie Chung asked him the question. "I have a competition problem, a competitive problem. I've got an angel on this side—he's my little devil on this side. The gambling incidents illustrated that, hey, I made a mistake. But if gambling affects my life or the way I play the game or jeopardizes my family—sure, I'd give it up in a minute."

His greatest guilt, he said, was that he hadn't told his wife—"the head of the household"—how much he had lost. "She's concerned that I don't make this a habit," he told Chung. "If it's something that's going to have us go opposite ways, fine, I won't do it. I've learned from my wife's perspective to bet ten dollars, twenty dollars, fifty dollars at the most."

And then Michael returned to the theme that had been obsessing him for the past few years. It was bigger than basketball, bigger even than winning—it was his humanity, and his right to be fallible. "Maybe it's time for other people to step in and live this lifestyle," he suggested. "I won't have a problem with that. I'm past the stage where I must live a perfect life—if that's what it takes, I'm not the man for you."

His current dream, he added, was to be invisible. "I'd love to go to an amusement park with my kids," he said. "I haven't done that in I don't know how long, and I miss it."

There was a wistfulness in his voice that suggested he knew such a day was not likely to happen soon. But there was no hint that he was about to retire.

*   *   *

No one who met James Jordan would have said he was fifty-seven years old. He looked more like Michael's brother than his father. And he had the energy of a teenager. But on July 22, 1993, he attended the funeral of a friend who had recently retired. Afterward, James said he was going to stop working and enjoy the rest of his life.

It was late when James Jordan left the home of friends in Wilmington, North Carolina. Although he had a two-hundred-mile drive home to Charlotte, he wasn't concerned—he had a shiny red Lexus sports car, ideal for the trip. But as he drove, he got tired, so he pulled into a highway rest area and, with the windows open, dozed off.

When he awoke, there was a .38-caliber pistol pointed at his chest. He panicked. So did the man with the gun. And in an explosion of violence that has become increasingly common in America, another life was snuffed out.

The alleged killers—two North Carolina eighteen-year-olds, one of whom had been arrested six times in the past two years—are said to have discovered almost immediately whose father they had killed. For that reason, police say, they hid the body in a swamp near the South Carolina border. Then they drove around, making calls on the cellular phone before hiding the car in the woods.

James Jordan liked to make road trips, so no one in his family was immediately aware of his disappearance. That weekend, Michael flew to Los Angeles and played in

Magic Johnson's annual charity game. It wasn't until early August that anyone became concerned.

Around the same time, the police found a body snagged on a tree limb in a South Carolina creek. It was so badly decomposed that identification was impossible and cremation seemed advisable. A few days later, a car was found, stripped and vandalized. It wasn't until August 12 that the Lexus was traced to James Jordan and the sheriff of a small South Carolina town came to feel that vehicle had some connection to the body he'd found. On August 13, the Jordans knew the worst.

Weeks earlier, newspapers reported that James Jordan had disappeared. With that, the rumor machine began working overtime. Maybe James had been kidnapped, word had it, because Michael had offended some important gamblers. According to the story heard in Las Vegas, Michael had received a phone call: "This is what happens when you don't pay up."

The report that two teenagers bent on robbery were in custody put an end to those wild stories but not to the pain of the Jordan family. The press was barred from funeral services in a small North Carolina church, where Michael wept as he spoke about the lessons he'd learned from his father. Michael smiled through the tears at the end of his reminiscence, but there was no mistaking his grief—he had lost his best friend.

The weeks of speculation in the press angered Michael almost as much as the murder itself. "Throughout this painful ordeal, I never wavered from my conviction that Dad's death was a random act of violence," he said in a statement on August 20. "Thus I was deeply disturbed by the early reports that there was a sinister connection to Dad's death. I was outraged when this speculation continued even after the arrests of the alleged murderers."

In the days after that, Michael played golf and avoided the press. He didn't seem to be preparing for the start of training camp in early October, but no one made anything of that. "He was really depressed last month," Charles Barkley reported in September. "Now he's starting to come around. He's excited for basketball to start, he's looking forward to the season. I think basketball will be a distraction from everything. Retirement? He never mentioned it. You can't quit living because something bad happens to you."

He could, however, quit playing basketball. That, he recalled, is what his father had urged him to do after the Bulls won their first championship. James Jordan had repeated that message last spring as they rode together in a limousine to Atlantic City. Now, with his father gone, the idea had more and more appeal. And what better homage to his father could there be than this: He saw me play my last game.

In September, Michael called Jerry Reinsdorf and told him that he wanted to retire. "I'm convinced you're doing the right thing," Reinsdorf said. "It would be dishonest for me to try to make you stay."

Michael next called upon Phil Jackson. "Do I have anything left to prove?" he asked his coach. Jackson thought for a moment and shook his head. Michael had done it all.

Michael didn't talk it over with his mother, who was in Kenya and knew nothing of his retirement until she read the news in an African newspaper. But he talked it over at length with his wife and his closest friends. They saw how he felt—unmotivated, angry, tired, restless. They couldn't, in good conscience, tell him he owed anything more to the sport or the public.

Early in October, it was a relaxed Michael Jordan who threw out the first ball at the league championship series between Reinsdorf's Chicago White Sox and the Toronto Blue Jays. And then, because Michael had told his teammates and word was starting to slip out, he and Reinsdorf invited the press to attend a news conference in the gym where he had practiced so diligently.

Michael wore a stylish tan suit, a crisp white shirt, and a conservative striped tie on the morning of that press conference. He sat between his wife and Reinsdorf, with Phil Jackson, his lawyer, David Falk, and the NBA commissioner, David Stern, flanking them. His voice was firm. And his statement was unequivocal.

He talked of motivation and challenge, and how there was nothing to inspire him to accomplishments greater than those he'd already recorded. "I always wanted to quit at the top," he said. "I never wanted to feel that foot in the back from others trying to push me out, saying I had got too old or that I couldn't do what I once could."

And, most of all, Michael talked of his father. He wasn't retiring because his father had died, he emphasized. He was leaving because he had learned—from his father's life and his death—that time is precious. "There are times when you have to put games aside," Michael said. "I wanted to give more time to my family. I've been very selfish about centering things on my basketball career. Now it's time to be unselfish with them."

Had the press contributed to his decision to retire? Michael said it hadn't. But when he finished speaking and reporters started asking questions, his mood changed dramatically. Now he was angry and defiant—and quite happy to unload on the media.

"I've always said I wouldn't let you guys run me out of the game," he began. Someone asked if he would become a broadcaster. "I would never do you guys' job," he snapped. "You don't have sympathy for normal people sometimes. I think I do."

Then what *will* you do now? someone asked toward the end. "I'm going to watch the grass grow," Michael said with a thin, edgy smile, "and then I'm going to cut it."

*　　*　　*

It wasn't that simple. NBC and Turner Broadcasting had just signed a six-year, $1.1 billion contract with the NBA that was scheduled to feature seventeen Bulls games the first year alone—would people watch those games if Michael was home trimming his lawn? In Las Vegas, the Bulls had been two-to-one favorites to win a fourth consecutive championship. Now those odds were readjusted to twenty-five-to-one—unless, of course, Michael decided to reappear later in the season. The value of the Bulls franchise, said to be $170 million when Michael was active, was estimated to have dropped by at least $25 million with his retirement—though it could regain that hefty sum overnight if Michael returned.

No one, it seemed, wanted to believe that Michael was really gone.

Michael showed up at one Bulls practice, just to watch, but his presence was a distraction and he didn't come again. On the last possible day, Michael gave the NBA formal notice that he wouldn't be playing this year. Then he once again put on his business clothes and told a television audience the fact it couldn't seem to accept.

"I do whatever I feel like these days," he told Oprah Winfrey in late October. "I knew at the end of the season I was going to retire. I tried to give subtle hints, but no one picked up. I was getting a bit bored. My game has changed. A lot of the air was being taken. I could still fly—there just wasn't as much opportunity."

He sounded at peace with his decision. But there was still something unconvincing about the idea of Michael Jordan, thirty years old and in peak condition, feeling fulfilled by playing catch with his children.

Michael apparently felt those same doubts, for he started to change the pattern of his days. Golf was no longer his only physical activity—now he went, every other day, to Comiskey Park. There, hidden in a tunnel, he took a baseball bat in hand and tried to hit balls thrown by a pitching machine.

For years, it had been rumored that Michael would become a professional golfer after he retired. "That's just a competitive dream," he had told me. "I put that up there so I have something to push me. I don't know if I'll ever get to that point. If I don't, I won't be disappointed. But I do need something to push me every day."

Golf was now fading, however. Baseball ruled. Many were surprised, but along the way, there had been hints. A few years earlier, Michael posed for pictures in a baseball uniform at Comiskey Park. Then he took batting practice. The Bulls general manager bet Michael he couldn't hit the ball out of the infield—whereupon Michael smashed ball after ball over the outfield fence. To top off that little show, he went into the bull pen and tried pitching. The radar gun clocked his fastball at eighty-five miles an hour, a speed that is just shy of respectable in the major leagues. And then, in 1993, Michael took batting practice before a stadium full of fans at the all-star game in Baltimore.

Early in 1994, Reinsdorf tried to play down reports of Michael's baseball ambitions. "If he was eighteen and you were scouting him, you'd say he has great tools—but he's thirty," Reinsdorf emphasized. "Michael never told me he wanted to go to spring training or play for the White Sox, but he loves being at the ballpark and the batting cages, so why wouldn't we let him? I know Michael well enough to know that he wouldn't do anything to make a fool of himself."

A month later, Michael made it clear that he intended to show up in Florida and see if he had the makings of a professional right fielder. White Sox executives were less than thrilled. "If I didn't bring him into training camp, someone else would," Ron Schueler, White Sox general manager, told reporters. "The odds are way against him—he's got a million-to-one shot."

Many baseball experts agreed. The fact is, Michael is really too tall for baseball. Because of his height, he presents pitchers with an enormous strike zone. And because he hasn't played competitive baseball since his junior year in high school, he lacks the quick eye, strong wrist muscles, and bat speed necessary to protect that strike zone. Michael can run very fast—his speed of 3.8 seconds from home plate to first base was the best on the White Sox team during spring training—but what does that matter if he can't hit?

In the field, Michael also had much to learn. At the start of spring training, he had trouble gauging the flight path of routine fly balls. Once known as "His Airness," he soon became dubbed "His Errorness."

And that was only the start of the criticism.

"I can shoot free throws," snapped New York Yankee slugger Wade Boggs. "Does that make me an NBA player?"

"I thought he wanted to escape the carnival of cameras and microphones. I thought he wanted peace and quiet. I thought he wanted to take his kids to an amusement park," wrote New York sportswriter Mark Kriegel. "Guess I thought wrong."

The ultimate came when *Sports Illustrated* put him on the cover—but urged him to end this foolish fantasy and quit baseball.

Through it all, Michael kept his composure. He arrived so early for batting practice that he was once spotted taking his cuts at 6 A.M. He played until his hands bled. And he never requested any special consideration.

"I'm not asking for a shortcut, I'm not asking for more money than anyone else in baseball," Michael said. "All I want is the chance to fulfill a dream I've always had. That's all I want to be judged on, whether I can play the game. If I don't have the skills, I'll walk away. I don't want to be a sideshow."

Even for the greatest athlete in the world, the transition from a fast-moving game with a big ball to a slow-paced contest with a mere pellet was very, very difficult. Despite all his work, he had trouble hitting. And he was still prone to error in the field. No one was surprised, therefore, when Michael was sent down to the Birmingham Barons, a farm team that traveled by bus and paid its players less per year than Michael used to make for half of a basketball game. "I lived in a situation where I had the world at my feet," Michael said. "Now I'm just another minor leaguer."

But he wasn't at all bitter—even about the criticism he was getting in the press. "Baseball began as my father's idea," he explained. "We had seen Bo Jackson and Deion Sanders try two sports, and my father said, 'You've got the skills. You could have made it in baseball, too.' He thought I'd proven everything I could in basketball. I told him, 'I haven't won a championship.' Then I won it, and we talked about baseball on occasion. And then he was killed."

So baseball has become Michael's way of keeping his father alive. Every morning, right after he wakes up, he says he has a conversation with James Jordan: "I talk to him more in the subconscious than in actual words. He tells me, 'Keep doing what you're doing. Keep trying to make it happen. You can't be afraid to fail. Don't give a damn about the media.' Then he says something funny— or recalls something about when I was a boy, when we'd be in the backyard playing catch like we did all the time."

These "conversations," Michael says, "take my mind away from what's happening and lift the load a little bit." They also contain advice that's useful for anyone, in any situation. For in these early-morning sessions, Michael hears James Jordan saying, "You never know what you can accomplish until you try."

Although Michael got off to a slow start at Birmingham, he continued to follow his father's advice. "I went down to visit him," says Walter Iooss, the photographer who has worked most closely with Michael, "and I happened to see him play when he had a wonderful night. He was two-for-three, three runs batted in, two stolen bases. After the game, Michael said, 'You know, if I keep hitting like this, they're going to have to move me up.' I said, 'Where? To Nashville [another White Sox-owned minor league team]?' And he goes, 'No, man! The big time— Chicago!' "

Michael's effort didn't pay off. He spent the entire season with Birmingham, where he was not exactly a superstar. For the year, he batted a less-than-respectable .202, getting 88 hits—and striking out 112 times—in 432 at bats. Playing right field, he made 212 putouts—and 11 errors.

In July, when Michael was in a long batting slump, a

rumor began to circulate that he would come to his senses and end this experiment in September, just in time to get in shape for the basketball season. Michael admitted that his disappointing performance had made him think of leaving the team but that his coaches had told him not to get discouraged. He made it clear, however, that even if he did quit baseball, he wouldn't be returning to the basket-ball court. "I don't like to close doors," he said, "but if you want me to say it, okay: 'I will *never* play basketball again, except recreationally."

Michael couldn't have been more direct. And yet the hope that he would put on a Bulls uniform erupted again in September, a few days after the minor league baseball season ended. The occasion was Scottie Pippen's All-Star Classic, a charity game held in Chicago to benefit Jesse Jackson's Operation PUSH. It was played in Chicago Sta-dium, the scene of Michael's greatest triumphs. And be-cause it was the last game ever to be played there—thanks in large part to Michael's impact on basketball in Chicago, the Bulls were trading in that old barn for a spanking new stadium—emotions ran even higher.

There was a sustained ovation when Michael stepped onto the court. And it was only the beginning of the cheers he heard that night. For although he hadn't played basketball in fifteen months, Michael was as great as ever. He began by charging past the foul line, faking to one side, and then, with no warning, lifting off for a dunk.

Later, he reenacted a dunk from his golden era, leaping from the foul line and roaring toward the basket. He shot three-pointers, reverse layups, fadeaway jumpers. Late in the fourth quarter, as the crowd chanted, "Michael! Michael!" he made Pippen think he was going to drive to the basket, then launched a jumper that swished through the net like a shot from one of his videos. Finally, with only a few seconds to play, Michael got down on his knees and kissed the Bulls logo at center court.

Michael got a standing ovation for that loving gesture, as well as for the fifty-two points he had scored. Everyone agreed that his game was still spectacular; many noted that, despite his layoff, Michael was still a better player than anyone in the NBA. And so, yet again, Michael had to bring fans and players alike back to reality.

He would soon be leaving Chicago, he told reporters, to go to a baseball instructional league, hoping that an improvement in his batting technique would help him in his quest to play on a major league team. "The game of basketball will always be a part of me," he said. "But I believe in myself and I believe in my dream. And I'll continue to follow my dream."

A traumatic death calls the meaning of life into question, and a grieving survivor often makes a radical change in his work or his relationships.

Committing himself to a second career that holds

every promise of failure is probably good therapy for Michael. Since his high school days, he programmed himself for excellence in one thing, and he had to exclude almost every other interest in order to be dominant in that one thing. It took a bullet to his father's heart to get his attention. What happened next is right out of a textbook—touched in ways too private to share, Michael needed to be as far away from the public as possible. He had to stop, take a breath, and see what else is in the world.

In choosing a dream that returns him to his roots, Michael honors the values he learned from his father and mother: hard work, honesty, humility. Whether he makes it to the major leagues or not, two facts are indisputable. Many people will be watching. And many more will be hoping he succeeds.

BIBLIOGRAPHY

$\mathbf{M}$ICHAEL JORDAN has been the subject of thousands of articles and a handful of books. I recommend David Breskin's profile of Michael in *GQ* (March 1989) and the following books:

The Golden Boys: The Unauthorized Inside Look at the U.S. Olympic Basketball Team, by Cameron Stauth (Pocket Books, 1992).

Hang Time: Days and Dreams with Michael Jordan, by Bob Greene (Doubleday, 1992).

The Jordan Rules, by Sam Smith (Pocket Books, 1992).

Rare Air: Michael on Michael, by Michael Jordan (Collins, 1993).

Swoosh: The Unauthorized Story of Nike and the Men Who Played There, by J. B. Strasser and Laurie Becklund (Harcourt Brace, 1991).

Taking to the Air: The Rise of Michael Jordan, by Jim Naughton (Warner Books, 1992).